Reading this book is like c̲ guy who sits on the back r̲o̲w̲ ̲i̲n̲ ̲G̲o̲s̲p̲e̲l̲ ̲D̲o̲c̲t̲r̲i̲n̲e̲ class smiling to himself as he does crossword puzzles on his phone so that you think he's not listening but who always comes out with the comment that turns the discussion into something bigger, something that matters. Jepson treats his characters—these glorious, quirky, hilarious young people trying to figure out their places in the world, trying to understand their own hearts—with humor, yes, but also with a subtle tenderness, so that we recognize their yearnings. This book is as fun as a pick-up game of Pictionary, but just when you think it's all Peanut M&Ms and Twizzlers, holiness appears as if on a silver tray passed by the deacons. The ending sneaks up on you like your home teacher (minister) on a unicycle bearing mint brownies, and, like him, is sweet and surprisingly healing. The sunset our Classic Protagonist rides off into is a different sunset than she had thought she was aiming for, a better sunset, and that makes all the difference. It makes this book true.

—Darlene Young
author of *Here*

Hilarious, subversive, reflective, and poignant, this novel is a revolving portrait that perfectly captures the BYU single experience and the internal and external tensions faced by Latter-day Saint women.

— Katherine Cowley
award-winning LDS author

Reading this lovely novel had me chuckling, nodding, and periodically gasping. Though BYU student Julie is the center (or at least an important context) of most of the action, we get to know the quirks and endearing phrasings of several others connected to her in some way. The book reminded me of Wilder's *Bridge to San Luis Rey*, wherein we get glimpses of several lives about to end (the bridge will collapse as they cross it), and of the events that led them to the bridge. *Just Julie's Fine* does not end with everyone's death, but with the compelling initiation of the title character into a new life—not the one she had always imagined. Julie, who is perpetually pursued by young Mormon men in search of a beautiful and (parenthetically) good wife, realizes that she wants [spoilers redacted]. This may seem like a simple thing, but it is a true rite of passage, a change of trajectory, and emblematic of the cultural changes happening around all of the characters.

Just Julie's Fine is also a fascinating time capsule in which we see BYU students grappling with the standard coming-of-age issues, but also with feminism, sexuality, faith, and duty.

I found every character to be likeable—except the counselor, who seemed vacuous. The clever dialogue felt real and inviting. The writing itself flowed beautifully.

This is a fun novel, and I think Jepson enjoyed writing it. The energy of FUN comes through in every page. It is not a comical novel, but the dialogue is often so witty that the reader will certainly smile. It's not a sad novel either. It's a slice-of-life novel wherein the reader gets introduced to a variety of fascinating characters who reflect their age and their time perfectly.

—Margaret Blair Young
author of *Salvador*

Just Julie's Fine

a novel

Theric Jepson

For information contact
By Common Consent Press
4900 Penrose Drive
Newburgh, Indiana 47630

Cover design: Matt Page
Book design: Andrew Heiss

www.bccpress.org
ISBN-13: 978-1-948218-96-2

Printed in the United States of America!

10 9 8 7 6 5 4 3 2 1

Contents

Meet Mary Sue

Good writers never make Mary Sue the hero of their story.

You know Mary Sue, I assume? The character upsettingly beautiful yet thoroughly humble. Can do calculus in her sleep yet would never embarrass Captain Kirk[1] if he figured the tip wrong. Chaste, but in a way that makes the boys admire her all the more.

Mary Sue.[2]

The character so perfect every reader hates her.[3] Or at the very least disbelieves in her. While in the fictional world all people, heroes and villains alike, adore her utterly.

---

1. James Tiberius Kirk (2233–2371)
2. Named 1973 by Paula Smith in her parodic short-short "A Trekkie's Tale," but birthed in prehistory. Perhaps it should also be mentioned that Mary Sues are, in the words of David Orr, "ludicrously empowered author prox[ies]," to get ahead of any smart-aleck reviewers capable of reading footnotes and feeling shame.
3. A reader of taste and refinement, that is, viz. you.

See why she makes a lousy protagonist? How are you supposed to identify with her?[4] How are you supposed to care when something "bad" happens to her? You the reader shall either hate her or be bored by her!

And yet here we go:

Julie Them.

First name Julie, classic and cute, unassailable. Last name Them. I can just about promise you you're saying it wrong, but would Julie ever correct you? No! Never! She's too sweet to even think it.

And besides, just Julie's fine.

Her nose is sloped just so and her cheekbones are just as high as they ought to be and this is America[5] so let's face facts and admit that it is very hard to be a Mary Sue unless you have just the right complexion on the fairest of skin, and our Julie has these as well, exaggerated by hair dark as cut moonlight.

She graduated from Fresno's Bullard High School with an unadjusted 4.0. She never had to work that hard for her grades, and her male teachers always bubbled in A DELIGHT TO HAVE IN CLASS on their gradesheets. A good Mormon girl,

---

4. Beautiful and humble though you be.

5. Julie qualifies as a good, American girl even when using the more stringent characteristics proposed by the late authority Tom Petty: She had been raised on promises; she loves Jesus (though she rarely thinks of him), her mother (though they rarely talk), Elvis (possibly ironically), horses (from a distance and really only in theory), and, if she had a boyfriend, one imagines she would love him as well. (She does not have a boyfriend.)

she took her pink skirts and shining hair to Brigham Young University where she signed up for the Marriage, Family, and Human Development major because the nice preregistration counselor suggested she should and so she just derived functions for fun on the weekends.

When she had time. Never did a Saturday feature fewer than two dates. Her dormmates: flabbergasted. They had never heard of a breakfast date before, and here was Julie invited to the Creamery for a breakfast of waffles and ice cream by a different boy every goshdarn Saturday. The only real question was how the boys would negotiate her afternoons and evenings. Would one boy take all the hours? Would they get divvied up among two or more suitors?

And thus passed her freshman year in the dorms.

Sophomore year, her bouncy blonde friends Maddysyn Windham and Ashleigha Lawrence invited her to join them in a blue brick house south of campus[6] that was advertising two open rooms, three open spots. They would share the two-bed room and Julie would take the one- and oh! you *have* to come, Julie, you *have* to! please! please! please!

And so she did.

Her room was basically a closet with a closet, but it was cozy and clean and painted a happy shade of not-quite-white pink. The house's third room was shared by locally reared goth[7] Anastasia Taylor who hated her parents, and Jilly King recently from Montana but really from Oakland.

---

6. Called Brick House because it "matters" in exactly the same way Netherfield Hall "matters" (movie version).

7. In her heart. Barely only sometimes in her makeup.

She was small and polite and looked fourteen, as quiet and dark as a shadow[8], a recent Mormon convert[9] who still felt disoriented without tall buildings[10] and was taking the prerequisites pursuant to nursing.

She wants to be a midwife because she fears she will never have children of her own. Which fear she has never told anyone.

But she will tell Julie.

Julie remains a good student and she gently corrects those who say MFHD is just for those looking to get an MRS degree[11] and explains all the valuable things she's learning and all the broad applications to those skills. The boys are embarrassed and apologize and think what a marvelous mother she'd be! and what are you doing Friday? how about Saturday? Tuesday? when when when are you next available?

And Julie smiles and touches their arms just above the elbow—and they know they will wait forever if they have to.

To know her is to love her. The only bad things to have happened to her are too many good things. When she walks

8. If you're not sure how to feel about this description, may I suggest discomfort? It's lovely and poetic, but it is also borderline racist. As soon as a story features a Mary Sue, other lazy tropes and stereotypes are sure to arrive.

9. In comparison to her presumably born-converted housemates.

10. The tallest building in Oakland is 404 feet tall and called the Ordway Building. Jilly has never heard of it either. In her memory, however, the buildings of Oakland are much taller and much more plentiful and . . . have you been to Montana?

11. This is a tired joke and has been for decades. I am pleased to assure you it will not recur within these pages.

down the street, birds call her name and the sun smiles more broadly.

I do not know how you will stand her.

You should be skeptical of these claims of course without some physical evidence, so let's dump her weekend purse out on the table and see what we see.

Nokia 6100: Dead. This is 2005 and it's become true that most college students carry cellphones. This particular phone was once Julie's mother's, and would work fine if Julie ever charged it. Which maybe she should. Her parents are paying $49.99 a month (plus taxes and fees) for her to have it in emergencies, after all.

Three tubes mascara, three tubes lipstick: The blue mascara she has never used, but her eldest brother once told her of a blue-eyelashed girl he'd briefly fallen in love with. The other tubes: her regular and a cheaper brand in case she ever needs to cry dramatically. The three lipsticks create the following effects: those lips!; those -gasp- lips!; (near loss of self-control).

Tissues: A small plastic sleeve, ever available to share with the needy, sick, or sad.

Tampon: In a cute light-green paisley plastic wrapper.

Moleskine notebook: Perfect-bound, grid paper[12], smallest size currently sold at Barnes and Noble, page edges markered pink.

12. Officially, Moleskine calls this paper "squared," but I worried you would feel I'm being intentionally abstruse. I want you to trust me—even though much of what I've said thus far must seem unworthy of said trust.

Pencils/pens: Usually kept in her pink weekday backpack, but on the weekends they migrate to her purse to keep her Moleskine company. Three hardnesses of pencil (including wooden and mechanical #2s) and seven different colors of pen, mixed Bic and gel.

Socket wrench: Kept for moments of distraction and, like the pens and pencils, most days of the week found in her pink backpack. Given to her by a high-school boyfriend's father[13] because it was perfectly weighted and she could spin it elegantly around her thumb or twirl it weightlessly through her fingers and he just felt she must have it.

Half-filled sleeve of Ritz crackers: Even Mary Sues must eat—but Julie has never lost crumbs to her tshirt and has never been unable to answer a question due to a too-full-of-crackers mouth. And she always has just enough to share.

Miscellany: No dust bunnies or used Q-tips or other nasty little fingernail-itchers that usually appear when a purse is dumped upside down. The purse is clean—almost hermetic—and smells like leather and daisies. Or, to be more accurate, like the sun shining off the leather belt of a beautiful girl lying in a halcyon meadow with no one but wildflowers and a poet as witness.

---

13. Did she love this high-school boyfriend's father's son? She told him she did, once, the day she left for college.

Meet The Twins

Hi! We're Maddysyn & Ashleigha! We grew up in Lehi and have been best friends *forever* and so of course we live together. We didn't last year when Maddysyn was in the dorms and Ashleigha was at home, but now we *do* live together! Yay! Even though Maddysyn's at BYU but Ashleigha didn't have the grades and so went to UVU, we totally don't judge each other and love each other so so much just like we always have! Besides. She can always transfer.

Now that we live in Brick House on Sixth East—or at least that's what Anastasia said its name is but isn't that weird? We think it's weird but Anastasia's been here a long time—she's getting like a master's degree or something—so she's the expert or whatever. But she's also always saying things like "Patriarchy sumthing sumthing" and how our hormones are like the opiate of the masses and that our apartment fails the Bechdel test—whatever that means. I think Anastasia's the reason Jilly never talks which is sad because she's the first African-American girl we've ever met and she seems really nice. And Anastasia's novels! We're sure there's lots of ess ee ecks in them. She has this one called *Incubus Dreams* (and we are *not* looking "incubus" up in the dictionary) where the cover girl's all hanging out of her negligee and she's wearing a blindfold. It's inappropriate. I don't know how we're supposed to feel the Spirit when she's reading those. We thought about throwing them out but she heard us talking and said it's unpatriotic to burn books what with this being America and everything which was mean because it almost made Maddysyn cry because her grandpa was in World War II or Vietnam or something and he's sick with some kind of cancer and might die anytime so Anastasia really shouldn't talk about America like that.

But we haven't even mentioned our favorite roommate who is Julie. Julie is *so* pretty. If we ever have plastic surgery it'll be to look more like Julie, or maybe to make our boobs bigger. She's the only one in Brick House with her own room and one time we walked in on her to borrow some mascara because she has so many kinds that she's never even opened and ours all got left open and dried out and she was changing and we forgot a little bit about charity because her skin is even more perfect than we'd assumed. And we'd assumed it was *hecka* perfect. And it made us remember this thing this only kinda pretty girl from the dorms once said that Julie oozes ess ee ecks (only she didn't spell it) which is a really gross thing to say when you think about it and made us feel dirty so we left the dorms and went over to Ashleigha's house and wrote an email to the Honor Code (which we didn't send because of forgiveness!), but we knew what she meant even if we're not friends with that girl anymore. Because Julie *likes* boys and *they* like *her* and so everyone's *thinking* about it even if they don't *know* they're thinking about it.

Which is, like, kind of good but kind of bad too? Because boys come over to see her and we get to meet them, but sometimes boys come over to see us but end up talking to her all night till we have to say, "Boys! Curfew!" and they have to leave because of the Honor Code which they do because Julie obeys rules—she's not one of *those*. Lately though, after they leave, she relaxes like so much. Her shoulders fall back and her neck rolls around and her eyes and mouth drop down a bit like she's melting and she sighs so long you think she'll run out of air and pass out or something. She used to be all bubbly and fun—we would talk all night—but now we have to wait until she *breathes* and *then* we start asking about the boys. She used to remember *everything*, but now she's started getting them mixed up and even started forgetting their names—but in the dorms? Julie was *famous* for knowing *ev*eryone's names on the first day! Before Maddysyn even knew her *roommate's* name! Julie was in the lounge doing these cheerleader tricks with this metal thingy and everyone was coming to watch her and she would point it at people and before anyone knew what was happening she knew everyone's name. She even bounced it off her hips once. You can't give boys a reason to talk about your hips that lasts *all year*. It's not fair! Really smart, but totally unfair.

On Tuesday, Anastasia noticed Julie wasn't remembering stuff and she was like, "Finally getting sick of all these dumb boys?" and Julie was like, "No, I like boys," and Jilly almost said something but she didn't so we jumped in and told Anastasia to mind her own business and that if she's ever going to get married she could at least *try* and then we told Julie which boys liked her best and which ones she shouldn't encourage and which we hoped would ask us out and asked how come she'd turned down Cute Paul Kyre for Saturday and she said, "Who?" so we just hugged her and told her to go to bed and she did because she knows we give good advice like that. And we owe her lots of good advice because she's the one we learned looking-over-the-shoulder-to-put-the-boobs-in-profile from. That's a pretty good thing to know, but if you just watch Julie you can learn lots of good things. Like bending your head and looking wide-eyed through your hair at someone. That one's supergreat.

The next night was Wednesday and Cute Paul Kyre came back and we were hoping he had come back to talk to us, but he just sat down on the couch next to Julie and he kept asking her questions like what's her dad do for a living ("office stuff") and how many siblings does she have ("two"). But she was reading some puzzle book and not really paying attention until he asked her what she was reading and she read him one about three men and two boats and a ton of bricks and a goat and not collapsing the boat and wolves on the shore or something confusing like that and Paul didn't know what to say so he sort of quiet-laughed and was kind of confused and it was pretty cute but also really irritating because we were sitting on the floor in front of him and we were wearing really cute tops that we knew would look really good from his position if he would just look down at them and we answered all his questions too and we gave way more interesting answers than Julie and really kept the conversation alive even when Anastasia who was sitting in her egg chair thing would turn a page in her dumb vampire novel and say rude things like, "Well la de da," and "Shocker!" We don't know if maybe she was being sarcastic or something, but why is it shocking if Ashleigha's big brother is a gym teacher at Highland? And if she *was* being sarcastic, why? She makes no sense. But either way we don't know if it was more her fault or Julie's that Paul left even though we were putting on lip gloss real slow and talking about how free our Saturday was looking and how bored we were and how cheap ice skating was at the Olympic rink if you bring your own skates (and we have our own skates). We were going to be in the Olympics once but then we got into horses instead and took equestrian lessons. Did you know that riding horses is totally good exercise? It is! And horses are so cute. And strong too. Sort of like Cute Paul Kyre we said like he couldn't hear but he wasn't listening. Other boys kept coming and sitting on the couch with Paul and Julie but then she would read them a puzzle about black and white hats or moving matchsticks or something and refuse to look at the end of the book for the answer so they kept getting embarrassed or frustrated or whatever and it was like the worst boy night ever. So the *next* night we put on our short shorts and our sports bras and a tank top and went jogging. Just a few blocks, just to make us all shiny. Because do we look really good just a tiny bit sweaty and our hair in ponytails? Yes, we do. We know because this one boy used to take pictures of us. He gave printoffs to us before he left on his mission which was hecka creepy but pretty sweet and really useful because we could see how cute we looked but also is why we don't wear yellow anymore even though it used to be our favorite color.

Anyway, we met these three boys and we jogged in place to keep our ponytails and stuff bouncing while we talked to them and invited them to our place. One was Parley and he is really sweet and cute even though he had a little zit on the tip of his nose and one was his roommate who was wearing leather pants which we didn't know people really did but we can see why people talk about it because he looked really good. The other guy was hot too and so we told them all to come over and then we ran home and took turns showering really fast and tried to decide which one we liked but it was a hard choice but it didn't really matter because only Parley came over. He said the other two had practice because they're in a band together which is *so cool* and Parley said maybe they could all come another time and we clapped our hands and said Yes! and he really did have a cute smile so we decided we liked him best and started elbowing each other trying to decide who should get him. But then of course Julie came in through the front door in this lumpy sweater that went all the way to her neck and Parley saw that and pretty much started drooling. At first she was just sort of polite in her new I-don't-really-care way but he kept trying and then he mentioned he interviews musicians and *then* she paid attention. She's been saying she wants to wear a mask and go to shows—we *know*, right?—and so she wanted to know who the best local bands were and since he knows them *all* he invited her to come over when he interviewed his roommate's band and of course she said yes and when he left she gave him a hug and we hadn't seen her give *any* boys hugs since Sunday at church (which counts but isn't the same thing) and we just stormed out of the room but we don't think she noticed because later she gave us some candy that her mom had sent her which was really good but there wasn't very much of it so we got out our ice cream and we all ate it together and watched part of *Sweet Home Alabama* together and when we fell asleep she must have put a blanket over us because when we woke up in the morning that's how we were. Jilly was eating breakfast and we had to hurry to get ready for school so Maddysyn could take Ashleigha so she wouldn't have to take the bus which is the worst.

Julie had already left so we just put a little heart sticker on her toothbrush.

She's the *best*.

Meet The Prattster

It would be unfair to suggest that I really "knew" Killer Trevor, but I did interview him clear back in 2005 before his first record deal, before the "incident" in Vegas, before the Tyler Glenn effigy, and certainly before his most recent accomplishment, punching Kanye West in the ear at the MTV Video Music Awards. In 2005 podcasting was a new medium and I was excited by it then—as indeed I still am. I interviewed Killer Trevor in my very first episode when I was just doing local music in the college town of Provo, Utah. Transcribing it now is an exercise in embarrassment, but I like to think I come off okay, and the interview was prophetic. I'm pleased that Jason has asked to include it in this Killer Trevor retrospective and I hope that it won't change anyone's opinion of me, my podcast Music Night Every Night (formerly—very formerly—The Prattster Show), or my current gig with Rolling Stone.

To set the stage for you, I was 21 and dumb as rocks. I'd convinced my roommate's band to be my first interview and I'd invited a girl over I'd hoped to impress. That second half of the equation is why I spent as much of my prep time arranging pillows on the couch as setting up my new recording equipment. Although lighting a cinnamon candle to cover up stale ramen and BO is never a bad idea.

I had blown my slush fund on bottles of water because I thought having them to offer would make me seem more professional. I don't know why I didn't think the five hundred dollars' worth of microphones could accomplish that, but I was a kid. Dumb as rocks, as I said.

So my roommate Teddy walks in with his band, Wyld Honeymoon Stallynz. I hardly knew the other guys, but I did know that they didn't look as clean-cut as your average student at Mormon-run Brigham Young University. Teddy had told me one member of the band hoped to get kicked out of BYU as part of his getting-famous plan. I assume that was Killer Trevor.

Happily, I had been testing the mics when Teddy opened the door and ushered everyone in, so I just let them run.

Enjoy!

Pratt Smithson
Ogunquit, Maine
June 17, 2014

Prattster: . . . levels looking good, testing, testing. Okay . . . Oh! Hey! Teddy! Stallynz! Great to see you. Thanks for coming over.

Teddy: Hey.

[Uncertain]: Hey.

Teddy: Car accident. He's fine, though. This is Parley.

Prattster: Parley Pratt Smithson! Parley by day, but call me The Prattster tonight. Working name! I'm expecting a friend to come help out, but no reason we can't get started. Have a seat. We should move these pillows. . . . Want a water? Okay. So here's the mic, one for me, one for you. It should pick you all up no matter what, but not a bad idea to lean in or hold it if you have a lot to say. Okay. Okay? Okay. So, before we start, I think this is important— Have you guys heard the *Provo Podcast*? I know we're not officially recording yet, but remember people can't hear you nod. Once we start, remember to say yes. Cool?

> [here they nodded, possibly spitefully—I've often wondered; possibly someone who insisted on being called "The Prattster" deserved a bit of spite]

Prattster: So the *Provo Podcast* is all—I mean, they do music and stuff too, but—they're all funny and stuff? *The Prattster Show* is more serious. Longform interviews? No stuff like film clips and, I don't know, skits and stuff. Just serious dig-into-the-music stuff. You—you brought your cd?

> [sounds of me fumbling then a few guitar chords as I successfully get the feed working from the player to whatever recording program I was using]

Prattster: Cool. You ready?

Various: Yeah.

> [the sound of a knock at the door]

Prattster: Hang on.

[here I went to get the door; I've tried to transcribe myself as accurately as possible]

Prattster: Hehh— Gkkk. Hhhhhh. Hi. Hi, Jujujujujulie. Hi, Julie. Hiya. Hiya, Julie. Hey.

Julie: Hey . . . John?

Prattster: P-Parley. Come in.

[in my wisdom and foresight, I'd had the band sit together on the couch which meant Julie had to sit by me on the loveseat; I don't know how I kept myself together with that kind of proximity—you can see what kind of 21-year-old I was]

Charlie: Holy Scheiß, woman! You fine!

Julie: I can leave.

Prattster: No no no no! Please!

Charlie: Sorry, babe. I mean, you. Miss. Something. I'm an idiot?

Prattster: That's Charlie. That's my roommate, Teddy. He plays bass. And that's Trev—"

Killer Trevor: Killer Trevor.

Prattster: Killer Trevor.

Killer Trevor: Hey.

Prattster: Julie, you're welcome to be part of this, Julie. But if you want to be, you can't wave on radio. You have to say something.

Julie: Of course. Thanks for letting me come.

Prattster: Um, heh heh. Yeah. Hee. Cool. Okay. Great. Um. Julie, we're just about to start, so—

Julie: Oh! hope I didn't keep you!

Prattster and Teddy and Charlie: No no no!

Julie: Oh good.

> [this part I remember perfectly, virgin that I was; she smiled and crossed her legs, leaned back into the arm of the love seat, threw an arm along the top, towards me, her shirt pulling tight around her, her hip pushing into the furniture; I was staring and I caught Teddy and Charlie staring—but Killer Trevor still hadn't even looked up; he was messing with his fingernails or something]

Prattster: Okay. Um. Let's start. . . . Ready? Okay. Let's go. Hellllllooooooo, music lovers! Weeeeelcome to *The Prattster Show*! I'm your host, The Prattster, and we're coming at you tonight live from Provo's surprisingly healthy music scene. With me tonight are cohost Julie, uh, Julie! and the town's newest enfant terribles Wyld! Honeymoon! Stallynz! who are already gaining a reputation for creative noise only a couple weeks since their first show. Bassist Teddy Jones, guitarist Charlie "Bob" Marley, and lead singer Trevor Lamont—

Killer Trevor: Killer Trevor.

Prattster: —welcome to the program.

Teddy: Thanks, bro.

Charlie: 'Sup.

Prattster: *The Prattster Show* is famed for its longform, unbridled interview format and tonight will be no exception.

> *[notice how cleverly I've avoided mentioning this is my first show]*

Prattster: So what say we start at the beginning? How did you guys first meet? Killer Trev. Tell us your version.

Killer Trevor: Killer Trevor. It rhymes and is like in iambs or something poetic like that. Cause I'm a poet. And that's what sets Wyld Honeymoon Stallynz apart.

Prattster: Makes sense. Killer Trevor. How'd you meet these guys?

Killer Trevor: I didn't *meet* them. I *chose* them. I go to five or six shows a week, looking for musicians skilled enough to perform my work. Think Tool, only more complex in its simplicity, performed with merely guitar, bass, drums.

Prattster: Who plays drums?

Killer Trevor: I haven't found a worthy drum player yet. So we do without.

Prattster: Okay. Charlie? Teddy? You must be flattered by Killer Trevor's descriptions of you?

> *[here we have a long pause as the two looked at each other silently negotiating who would go first, which gave Killer Trevor time to move back in, which led to them slomo collapsing into the couch and just letting him talk]*

Killer Trevor: They have talent, but we're still working on the specific skillsets needed for this music. So our first three shows have been lacking but they'll get better. Our fourth show is Friday. We'll be playing with My Bloody Fingers and The Eden Express and some other schmuck. I expect when people hear us juxtaposed so closely with The Eden Express, our ascendancy will be assumed.

Prattster: Eden's one of the best bands in town.

Killer Trevor: Only because kids don't know better. They will.

Julie: What about the other band you're playing with? How're they?

Killer Trevor: An astute question. I actually admire My Bloody Fingers. Just a trio of chicks of course, but, then, if she were available I'd put Meg White on drums. What other band in this Mormon town would dare have a band name that references both menstruation and masturbation? Color me impressed. Color me impressed.

Julie: Gross.

Killer Trevor: [*chuckles*]

> [*and winks, I might add; since finally looking up and noticing her, he'd been raising his eyebrows and his chin and doing all sorts of flirty facial bits; I was seriously regretting putting her in eye contact with him and not me; she stuck her tongue out at him around this time which about made me want to kick him—crazy how much I'm remembering as I type this stuff up*]

Prattster: So I haven't heard My Bloody Fingers yet. They've only been playing about as long as you. What do they sound like?

[I assume he made some gesture here]

Prattster: Well, what about the rest of you? What local bands do you like? OK Ikumi? I know Teddy likes OK Ikumi.

Killer Trevor: Ambient rock? All oxymorons shall fail.

Prattster: Destination Tokyo.

Killer Trevor: Self-indulgent, off-key—but I don't want to say anything else. Dude's my friend.

Prattster: Robot Ghost?

Killer Trevor: Please. My ears friggin' bleed.

Prattster: The Heaters?

Killer Trevor: The Heaters? You serious? The Ramones already played that schtick into the grave, thank you very much.

Prattster: Um, um, um, Mary Cox & the Pop Rocks?

Killer Trevor: *[after laughing loud, hard, and over fifteen seconds]* Seriously? That twee crap? It's just flirty folk pop in the overdone Provo tradition. I mean—"Republican Boyfriend"—is that supposed to be subterfuge?

Julie: What do you think about Mathematics Et Cetera?

Killer Trevor: Mathematics Et Cetera is Radiohead if Radiohead had no respect for itself.

> *[even then he could be a condescending prick—not that this should shock anyone]*

Julie: Oh, come on! Even I know Mathematics Et Cetera and they are awesome. Maybe better than Radiohead. And I've seen them *both* live.

Killer Trevor: Well thank you, darling, for proving my point. They're preoccupied—desperate for the mainstream. C'mere and I'll show you what I mean.

> [sounds of bandmates being shoved aside making just enough space for Julie to squeeze between him and the couch arm; I remember their jeans were so close in color I couldn't tell where one leg ended and another began; today, remembering her cross the room to Killer Trevor—Killer Trevor!—feels even more like one of my life's great failures]

Killer Trevor: Radiohead.

> [he shook her index finger]

Killer Trevor: Math Club.

> [he shook her bird then took her hand into his and began manipulating it as he made his "points"]

Killer Trevor: Your fingers are parallel. And without fingers, all pointing up and down parallaxly, we can't see how special and radical the thumb is. Yet without it, your hand is worthless. And that's music. Go back over there.

Julie: Okay.

> [she didn't]

Killer Trevor: I'll tell you who wasn't too bad. Sunfall Festival. You know they were on Conan? Not bad, not bad.

[I'm cutting out about thirty minutes here because it gets completely off topic consisting, as it does, primarily of Killer Trevor deliberately ignoring a pretty girl I'm trying to impress; diverting in its way I suppose, but not the sort of thing Jason wanted when he asked for this, I'm quite sure]

Prattster: Okay. So. Anyway! Back to the Stallynz. Dylan's always said that creativity is, like, ineffable. But you're pretty smart. Can we dissect one of your lyrics?

Killer Trevor: Sure. Hold your own hand.

[sounds of Killer Trevor standing and crossing the room to collapse next to me, leaving Julie and her hand bereft, I'm sure]

Killer Trevor: This is a remarkable new thing I'm working on. Not finished yet, so it's what you might call an unprecedented glimpse into the artist's process.

Prattster: So I'm unfolding a piece of paper that Killer Trevor's handed me. It's, uh, haha, really . . . well . . . folded. Okay. Here we are. It's just a standard eight-and-a-half-by-eleven piece of collegiate. Bit of the fluffy stuff still on the side where it was ripped out. Let's see. . . . No title?

Killer Trevor: Titles are so bourgeoisie.

[say what you will about Killer Trevor, at least he doesn't drop that word anymore]

Prattster: Okay. Cool. Shall I . . . read it?

Killer Trevor: Knock yourself out. Hey. You guys should listen up. This is our new number.

Prattster: Okay. Here we go. It starts here? Okay. Good.

> People in this house
> So many people in this house
> Black and brown and yellow
> People in this house
>
> People in this room
> Just some people in this room
> Just a bunch of whities
> Motherfu—

Hang on.

Killer Trevor: That's the way it is with art, man. People don't realize that around here, the truth is ugly. Always. Truth is always ugly. That's how you know it's the truth.

Julie: Tautology.

> *[I didn't know that word in 2005—hearing it here and understanding it for the first time, I wish I'd had the guts to put up a bigger fight for this girl's attention. But that's rather a romcom-style anti-feminist sentiment, isn't it? Don't tell Beyoncé I said any of this. I've yet to hold an uncanceled interview with her]*

Killer Trevor: When I look and all I see are a bunch of Mormons hiding their heads in the sand? We can't do that. We have to be honest. And music is the only way to get people to listen to my honesty. But keep reading. That was the regular rhythm and rhyme part. In the next part I start messing with time signatures.

Prattster:

> If you livin in
> A Mormon town like the fools that
> You are cuz
> We're all fools but I know and he
> Knows
> It and she knows
> It and he knows
> It but you are the fool the Mormon
> Fool you must listen
> Rabbits and sunshine and songs shall all die
> Yo, I'm amazing
>
> *[if you're wondering how I remember the line breaks, I don't—he has scans of these early lyrics in his Twitter feed if you look hard enough; sadly though, since I was reading, I didn't get to look at the band or at Julie, though you can bet he was thinking about their reactions . . . okay, her reaction]*

Killer Trevor: And that's what a complex honesty looks like. Water.

Prattster: So . . . how do you, um, propose to redeem . . . Mormons?

Killer Trevor: Can't be done. No hope. Impossible. Thanks, baby. You're too kind.

Prattster: Please, please sit down, Julie. Careful! Wires! Please?

Killer Trevor: She's cool. She's cool. But as I was saying, Mormons are irredeemable. There are exceptions though.

Me, for instance. The band's coming along. But as a whole? No. Lost cause. That's why I named the band Wyld Honeymoon Stallynz. I'm referencing two things. First, the greatest band within the milieu of the *Bill & Ted* universe in order to reflect their quaint form of satire and innocent faith in a future informed by rock and roll and John Lennon's "Imagine," easily the most important philosophical statement of the last hundred years. Second, I'm referencing that brilliant new movie *Napoleon Dynamite*, made by a couple of BYU students who abandoned the faith in order to make great art, as symbolized by the use of Elvis Costello's most heretic pseudonym. Huge props to them abandoning the staid mores of their Mormon past. Huge props.

Julie: So you're going to leave the Church?

Killer Trevor: You don't have to "leave the Church" to be an artist, but of course it helps. I'm staying on the tightrope though. The balancing act keeps me grounded and helps me soar through the introduction of breakable boundaries. So no.

Prattster: I'm pretty sure the Hesses—

Julie: Hang on just a second.

[sound of door opening and closing]

Killer Trevor: Anyway. Back to the song.

Prattster: They still—

Killer Trevor: Back to art, the contrast between house and room reflects the contrast between the colors of people in the world and the homogenous hive mind of Utah Valley.

Prattster: But *Napole—*

Killer Trevor: [*sighing impatiently*] Exactly. Just as Napoleon brought a brown horse to the wedding between his brother and a brown woman. The wild honeymoon stallion. Wild—a rejection of past mores. Honeymoon—this moment of history in which we have a chance to make a new start. Stallion—it will require all our animal might. Animals. Symbol of sexual strength of course. Animus. More poetic crap in other words. Stuff most people can't appreciate.

Prattster: Thank goodness Julie stepped out.

Killer Trevor: Yes. Most women, Mormon women, fear their own sexual power. Don't tell me that girl doesn't have power.

Prattster: So you ... sexual power ... ?

Killer Trevor: Honor code, man. I haven't decided that I shouldn't just get my degree before I go. Could be useful someday.

Prattster: What's your major?

Killer Trevor: Pre-med biology. Only way my grandma would pay for school. Have to disappoint her, though. I mean—I'm not gonna be a doctor, but at least I could finish the BS. If you know what I mean.

Prattster: Does, uh, does, uh, your science—

[*the door again*]

Prattster: Oh, hey, Julie. Do your science studies affect your music?

Julie: You're a scientist?

Killer Trevor: Sort of I am. Sort of I am.

Julie: Explain.

Killer Trevor: Sit down. There you go. That's nice. See, whether you're a god person or no, nature rocks. Take your lichen, right? What, a fungus and an algae living together? That's kuhrazy! We could learn so much from that. So to answer your Q, Parley—

Prattster: Prattster.

Killer Trevor: —here's a new song for you, a cappella, improvised, to give you a sense of my process.

> Lichen
> O!-o!-o! lichen can't you see
> The whole world could live like you and . . .
> Lichen
> O! o! o! lichen now I see

And so on like that.

Prattster: Wasn't that a Cat Stevens melody?

Killer Trevor: Rough draft man. It's all theft. Aren't you the one that mentioned Dylan? Dude stole the first five years of his career. It's all process.

Prattster: Your process is stealing stuff?

Killer Trevor: Homage, man. Homage.

Prattster: But you—

Julie: C'mon, Parley. Don't be mean. It was just off the top of his head.

Killer Trevor: Listen to her.

Prattster: Prattster....

Killer Trevor: Cool! Well, we done here? Cause I'm feeling good to go. Wake the band, pop some Dexedrine, get in a couple hours of practice. Let's go, guys! Get up! Up! Let's go!

[mumbling and moaning]

[stumbling]

Prattster: The cords! The cords!

[opening and closing of door]

Julie: Well! That was fun!

Prattster: Yeah. Hum. You—you want to come for my next one?

Julie: Maybe. Who is it?

Prattster: I—don't know yet.

Julie: Well. Let me know. When are those guys playing?

Prattster: Friday. Rootbeeragogo.

Julie: Great. I want to know if he's, you know, full of it. Maybe I'll see you there?

Prattster: Maybe....

Julie: Welp! See you later!

[opening and closing of door]

Prattster: Hhhhhhhhhhhhhh. Well. That sucked.

I'm still friends with Teddy on Facebook. He went on to be a CPA, believe it or not. Don't know if he's still wearing the leather pants. Killer Trevor, you know (God help you); Charlie, I don't. Julie—I've thought about Julie a lot over the years. Not sure what it was about her that's kept her in my mind while simultaneously preventing me from running her down. Should've at least have gotten her last name.

But at least she wasn't on Killer Trevor's arm at the VMAs. Let's call that a victory.

-ps-

Meet Heather the Bassist

Hi, Mom. Sorry to be writing at three in the morning. I guess it doesn't matter to you, but I have a feeling this email's going to be long so I guess it matters to me since I have school tomorrow. You need to stay up later so I can just call you. Anyway, I made a new friend tonight and a new enemy, and I think my friend will choose my enemy over me. Melodramatic enough?

First though, I think I'm getting better at that sort of Kim Deal purity of bassline. Clean as Eden's snow, like Grandma used to say. Though she wasn't talking about dun dun dun dun dun dun dun. I don't know why I'm telling you all this. You probably don't care. You probably wish I had a boyfriend instead of a bass. (But at least I type emails with proper caps and punctuation! Even at 3am. You succeeded there. Good job, Mom. Now how about sending an extra hundred a month?)

My band played tonight. We weren't supposed to start till 11, but I got there around 9 so I could do most of my getting ready before the opening band played.

Mary was there too and she was arguing with some guy wearing just a tasseled leather vest and too-tight vinyl pants. Greg, who runs the place, was trying to get between them. The guy was saying that even though he'd never played at Rootbeeragogo before, his band still should get top billing and go last. Basically, he was saying *we* should open for *him*. Which I could understand if he were Les Paul or somebody, but this guy's played less shows than us! No way he can push us off! Then he tries to "compliment" us by saying something totally nasty about our band name—which, sorry, Mom, I'm not repeating.

Mary: We're My Bloody Fingers BECAUSE I PRACTICE MY GUITAR.

Him: That's cute that you practice guitar. I play guitar.
?????

I almost hit him over the head with my bass case. I might have, except I'd just finished my portrait of Suzi Quatro in Wite-Out and no way was I smearing it on his pinhead.

Of course, Greg took our side and stuck with them going on first.

They weren't that great. They only had six songs and none of them really worked. They should stick with 3 chords until they learn how to structure a song.

During the set I was sitting at a table next to this girl with a kitten mask over the top half of her face. She saw my case so asked if I was playing tonight, then what the band

name meant, so I told her about Stevie Ray Vaughan super-
gluing his callouses and she nodded and said good in a way
that made me wonder if she'd heard the "other" meaning so
I asked if she knew the band playing. She said she "sorta"
met them yesterday. And what did she think of their music?
She didn't know, didn't think she "got" it. I told her there
wasn't much to get. It was just art-school crap. She laughed
and said she thought so too. We ended up chatting through
the rest of their set. Her name's Julie and she's awesome.
And smart. She explained the physics of harmony to me
on a napkin. Can you believe that? And it made way more
sense than in Mr. Wooten's physics class. I kept the napkin.
She made the waves and these little smiley faces as they
went up and down—it's hard to explain. Made me want to
take science again though, which should make you happy.
But I won't, so. . . .

After the set, Julie wanted to go talk to the band and I decided to go with her even though John White was playing
next and I probably shouldn't tell you this but he's super-
cute. Somebody told me he's married, but I don't think so.
I've never seen a ring, anyway.

The three guys in the band and some other guy were at
the bar drinking lemon waters (which Greg always gives
us thinking it's generous or something) when we came up
to them. Even with her mask on they all recognized her
immediately. Maybe she always wears a mask? The guy in
the vest ignored her but the other three were all Julie! Hey
Julie! Did you like the show Julie! So nice to see you Julie!
etc. No one even noticed me. Julie's pretty honest though

and said she didn't really get the songs and the guy in the vest said it's because "these retards" can't stay in time. I'm pretty sure they were just crappy songs, but the band didn't defend themselves.

Then he said, Julie! C'mere! The other guys looked at him like kicked dogs. Julie rolled her eyes and gestured for me to follow her. Which I did. So I was there the whole time. He never noticed. Curse of the bass player, Mom. Curse of the bass player.

Anyway, he was a jerk to her the whole time but she maybe liked it? Not that she seems like the abused type—it was more like she was . . . sick of people being nice to her? I don't know. Whatever.

The guy was just such a

Well. If Grandpa met him, he would say a*****e, and this is one time Grandpa would be right. That's exactly what he was. Strutting around in his vest, winking at girls who walked by, flexing his pecs, touching his nipples through the leather. Disgusting. I asked Julie about it later and she liked how he was trying to impress the girls walking by instead of her.

?????

Anyway, we watched John's set together from the bar then I went backstage to find Mary and Gertie.

And our set was AWESOME! We had everybody out of their seats and they made us play two encores! Which was great because Mary let us try my song out and it went pretty good. No third encore but that's probably not my song's fault.

After we packed up, I let Mary and Gertie drive off when I saw Julie talking to vestboy at the edge of the parking lot. I walked over and he was trashing us, but I don't know—"stuck in the old blues" hardly strikes me as an insult.

I said, "Hey, Julie. Let's walk home."

She shrugged and said, sure.

He said, "I thought I was taking you home?"

She shook her head. "You never asked."

"I shouldn't have to."

?????

It was like ten blocks to her apartment and the bass gets heavy but it was worth it. She knows a lot about music. Did you know Johnny Cash took one voice lesson and his teacher told him to never let anyone change the way he sings? But even though she knew that story, when I started singing "Ring of Fire" she didn't recognize it. But the weirder thing was that I thought she was going to thank me for helping her escape from that guy, but now I actually think she likes him. I mean, all she said was he's the first boy besides her brothers who isn't supernice to her all the time, but she was smiling when she said it. It's easy to believe everyone's nice to her, but who gets sick of people being nice?

Anyway, we got to her place and she let me in. A roommate was on the couch reading one of those vampire-hunter books you took away from me in high school, but she perked up when I pulled out the bass and plunked out a couple Cash tunes for Julie.

Her name's Anastasia like in the cartoon and she studies Sanskrit (Sanskrit!). It's hard to tell if she likes Julie but she definitely resents how many *boys* like her. She makes jokes, but it's pretty obvious.

I'll tell you though, listening to Anastasia's stories about the parade of boys? It made me all neurotic. Whenever Julie decides she's ready to settle down, she can have pretty much anyone she wants. But what about me? When I'm ready? And if someone like Julie can pick an idiot like vestboy, who might I end up with?

Eventually, Anastasia complained that all we were talking about was boys. Which was funny but kind of true. I gave Julie a hug and packed up. My house was six blocks back, but I like walking early morning when the streets are asleep. I walk in the road where I can see the stars without tree branches blocking the view. (Or tree roots tripping me. Dang Provo sidewalks.) Cassiopeia was high in the sky. I still think she looks like a crooked smile. Made me think of you.

To sum up. New friend. New a*****e. Temporary sadness. Will you be home after church on Sunday? I'll call. Pet Tabs for me. Make her purr.

Love you.

ps: about that hundred bucks

Meet Killer Trevor

You know how it is when people can't recognize your genius? Most people can't, having no genius, but *you* do. You know *exactly* what it's like to be surrounded by inferiors. Trying to be generous to them, giving them opportunities to be part of something bigger than themselves, but it's not easy to make them see. Geniuses just don't speak the same language as most people. And thus most people can't see how lucky they are to sit down with you. Break some bread. Play some music. It's not their fault, but that doesn't make them any less frustrating.

You have a few little techniques to subtly alert them to their fortune. For instance, bursting through doors, letting them crash against the wall—in old houses like this one, the windows rattle. Should shake plebes from their humdrum. Not an invitation they'll *all* recognize, but you give it to them anyway. You recognize that privilege is accompanied by responsibility. And some drama. Make their lives worth living, give them a story to tell. They knew *you*.

So you throw open the door. Being a girls' house, they don't expect you to enter without knocking. The crash and shake is just gravy. The girl you came for and her goth and black roommates had just been sitting around reading and now they look at you with huge wide eyes. A bit comical, really. You allow yourself the luxury of a brief smirk. You know it only adds to your look with hair all over the place and your shirt inside out and your jeans torn and your cowboy boots muddy. One thing you've learned from watching Stones footage is that looking a mess is part of the appeal. Maybe it's the mothering instinct? Genius doesn't need to understand itself. As long as girls are screaming your name, what's the difference?

You bark her name and invite her to talk. You keep your sentences under three words.

She closes her book, some big textbook, offers you the couch.

You suggest her room.

She counters front yard.

Not an argument worth having. Let her lead you out and, no, it's too early to slap her denim-painted ass. Just watch it, then slam the door as hard as you can so the girls left behind remember you, then jump at the girl from the top of the steps, landing close enough that one bending knee will pass between her legs. Sure, she takes a step back and crosses her arms, but she'll remember.

She tries to forget her flush of emotion with a simple

"What's up?" You counter with a hand run through your hair and notice with pleasure it's your own grease that keeps it standing. Time to broach the subject on your mind. You ask if she remembers that film you once admired, whose directors you once saw as equals.

She doesn't, so you spit on the grass. And say the name of the movie, *Nappy D*. No response. *Napoleon Dynamite*?

Now she remembers.

You'd just read an interview with them, learned they're still Mormon—going to church and everything.

She seems happy about this. She's missing the point. She doesn't get it. You'd liked that movie! You'd named your *band* after that movie! Now people will think you're just riding some sort of Mormon bandwagon! Trying to fit in. Which is not something minds like yours do. You stomp at a brown patch of lawn, digging in your heels, making divots of brown and green and brown. Fitting in is not you. You're your own man. Always have been. But now you'll need to prove it. So you're quitting the band you started and going solo. You're moving to Salt Lake. Then maybe Denver. Or Vegas.

She wants to know if you're dropping out of school. Of course you are. And so is she.

She's not bright enough to follow your meaning immediately so you have to explain. You tell her she *fits* you. You explain how rare that is. No one else in this town fits you. But *she* does. *She* can see your potential. *She* appreciates how talented you are. *She* would never hold you back. *She* can visualize how famous you'll one day be and it doesn't even make her jealous! Plus, she's beautiful which is something you'll need in a mate. Maybe you can buy her a tambourine and the two of you can find fame together.

She just looks at you so you go back to digging holes in the lawn while you wait. The best she can come up with is to ask if you're leaving the Church.

At first you say no, then admit you don't know. But who cares? If there's a god, he made you what you are: a genius. So if it makes her feel better, she can dedicate your success to God. Whatever. It's like—thinking you have to wear garments on stage.

Of course *that's* what catches her attention. Just like the band. We're returned missionaries, they said. We made covenants, they said. They don't get that you have to prioritize the music or you'll never show up.

She's not making any connections. But other people can be slow. It's important to be patient. Telling her to think about it's not going to suffice. You've been down this road before. Explaining. It's your curse. But it's part of the territory of being a step above. So you tell her: garments go to the knees—cover the chest and the shoulders. You remind her that she's seen you perform. That you wear a vest and pants and boots. Nothing else. Part of your job is to serve the ladies. If they can't see your chest or the shape of your ass, you're not doing your job. You're a rockstar. You can't wear garments and do your job.

She folds her arms and gives you a look you can't immediately decipher. She asks what you need her for, remarks that you seem "pretty set."

No! You shake your fists and step closer. She's missing

the point. This is a ride you'll take together. Her fandom is the evidence you've needed, the proof that you are what you've always known yourself to be. It's not shameful to admit she "made" you or to admit you can't leave her now. Perhaps you shouldn't have said it, but it's out and looking back isn't your style. What matters is the next wall to be knocked down between you and your future.

"I thought you were different."

This catches you off guard. Of course you are. That's the point.

She turns east and faces the mountains and says, "No. Not like that."

You don't know what she means but likely neither does she. You repeat your claim to genius and proclaim your need for her. You grab her shoulders and pull her to face you. After all, now you can't start without her.

"I know, I know."

You tell her that from the moment you first sat by her and took her hands—

"I have slut hands. It means nothing."

Which is proof she *does* understand you. You stutter in excitement as you proclaim again her compatibility for you. You hate yourself for coming off like a rube, but all you can do is stand to one side and listen to nonsense coming out of your mouth. You're talking about Sophie B. Hawkins. Her music's poppy shit, but she'll sleep with anyone! male! female! You can hear yourself dropping exclamation points like phat beats, but you can't hold up, the rhythm has you, the rhythm of your effin heart as that pathetic thing considers for the first time that you might lose her, that you're looking like a fool in front of her. But whatever. She's proof that the future's less about the quality of your work—it's what you stand for that matters. And she stands for sex and freedom and a good groove and those things that will last forever. Sophie may be shit but her stuff will last forever. Because of what she stands for. Because of what this girl stands for. It's something you've imagined but never believed before she practically sat in your lap. You're saying this, you're hearing yourself saying this, you're hating the fact that your virginity's showing. In front of her.

You tell her the two of you matter. You *matter.*

"I don't—"

You place a finger on her lips to shush her. You tell her you're going to kiss her now, right here, on this street, in front of her house, and that anyone who sees you will know that the two of you are not trapped in their petty world. If you separated lips long enough to tell them you're moving to Salt Lake together and playing clubs and changing the world they wouldn't even be surprised.

And then you press her to you. For a second, you feel her arms tense like she might slap you, but then she relaxes and you let go of her shoulders and explore her hair and back and waist. Then you pull back and tell her to grab what she needs and you can hop on a bus and go.

She sort of nods and regards you. She finally understands.

"You know," she says, "for a sec, I was worried you might be a good kisser." Then she turns and walks up the steps and through the door to her house. You watch it close and hear her draw the deadbolt.

You know how it is when people can't recognize your genius. You just have to walk away, and prove them wrong. Again. And again. And again. And again. And again.

Meet Bram Stoker

Emory Van Doren was certain Anastasia knew he was gay. Since no straight man could resist her roommate's siren charms, she would never have invited him to Brick House otherwise. That said, the first time he walked through the front door and past the two volleyball players (Emory did not care for sports, but he never missed a men's volleyball game and thus recognized Mel Jacoby and Thomas Young immediately) vying for the attention of the, granted, unusually pretty girl sitting across from them upon the couch, he, in accordance with deliberate habit, quietly catalogued her attributes and compared them against the mental catalogue of Pretty Girl Traits he kept on file, in case he were later conscripted into a growlingly masculine conversation of objectification:

Legs: smooth, long, "shapely" (?), in shorts short enough to be shorts but long enough to allow plenty of mystery

Arms: lanky yet elegant

Breasts: bags of fat draped in a loose fitting tshirt (luckily for Emory, Mormon boys at Brigham Young University generally find breasts too spectacular to speak of)

Neck: long enough to be expressive, short enough to remain . . . demure?

Face:

Here, Emory's words had failed him. She was not merely pretty. She was—the platonic ideal of human. Inasmuch as such a thing is possible. Then he'd felt Anastasia smirking at him from across the room and the moment passed. He'd walked over and sat on the floor next to the chair Anastasia sat in and had said, "I see what you mean," before directing his attention to the smooth, long, elegant Mel.

Today they sat together again—Anastasia in her ratty student-house armchair, Emory on the floor beside her, both of them utterly invisible—and whispered awe-filled comments back and forth as they watched Julie deal with two new fine-looking men.

Anastasia: "See how she tilts her head to the side just so and they subconsciously mimic the move?"

Emory: "She let a full twenty seconds pass between question and response! I could never be that brave."

Anastasia: "I've seen her let a full twenty *minutes* pass. No joke. This guy asked her out and she finished the *Lestat* I'd lent her before saying, 'Sorry.' I about pissed myself."

Emory: "I keep forgetting you hate her."

Anastasia: "Only possible when I'm not in the same room with her. Promise you'll hate her when you leave."

Emory: "Every nymph is jealous of Aphrodite. Only the most foolish dare hate."

Anastasia: "I could have sworn you told me you were a fool."

Emory: "Different subspecies. Look at that: I never realized holding a pen could be sultry. Does she give lessons?"

Anastasia: "You should ask. The boys would love that."

Here, Emory said nothing. Although many of the gents he hung out with were as out and proud as possible while remaining at BYU, he had never told them he too was gay. He was completely open in his own mind, but with others he settled for silence. No doubt, he assured himself, out of respect for the tender sensibilities of innocent roommates who had no idea they'd ever met a gay Mormon. Such innocence! Much too beautiful not to preserve.

"She likes vampires?"

"Hmm?" Anastasia looked up from her copy of *Blood Canticle*. "Not particularly. She seems to like socket wrenches. I did try to turn her onto Ms. Rice but it didn't take. More urgently, I'm thinking of reading *Varney the Vampire*, have I mentioned?"

Emory raised an eyebrow. "Do you have any idea how long that is?"

"It's not like I have to finish it. But I ought to at least try. It's pretty much the source for modern vampires—like, fifty years before *Dracula* or something. Besides, if I hate it, I'm back to Laurell Hamilton quicker than Anita Blake drops her panties."

"Charming."

"What do you know about vampires, anyway?"

"I've been looking at Bram Stoker for my thesis."

"You're studying Whitman."

"And Stoker was a huge fan. Huge."

"Really?"

"Yeah." Emory watched Julie's suitors cross their legs in unison, matching a movement she had made a few seconds before. Frankly, they did it better. "Who do you think Dracula's based on?"

"Shut up."

"No. Look at this." Emory lugged his bag onto his lap and pulled out a spiralbound notebook. "Listen: 'There lay the Count, but looking as if his youth had been half renewed, for the white hair and moustache were changed to dark iron-grey; the cheeks were fuller, and the white skin seemed ruby-red underneath; the mouth was redder than ever, for on the lips were gouts of fresh blood, which trickled from the corners of the mouth—'"

Emory closed the notebook on his thumb and waved it at Anastasia. "Granted, Walt probably never leaked blood from his mouth; the important thing's the hair and the moustache and the tall and the sexy. Sound like anyone you know?"

"That's pretty weak evidence, E. So Drac's quote-unquote Whitmanesque, but how was Whitman like a vampire? Besides his sexy 'stache, I mean? You do know Whitman did not invent white hair?"

Emory held a fist to his heart. "It's the attraction factor. Walt Whitman attracted people. He had a . . . draw. Like a benign vampire."

"What would be the point of a benign vampire?" She took his notebook from him and looked through his notes. Emory wondered if her Sanskrit studies helped with interpreting his handwriting. She flipped it over and handed it back to him. "So you think Stoker was gay?"

Emory took his notebook. "No, no. It wasn't like that. But he *was* attracted to Walt—as a poet, as a man. As, like, an archetype of what manliness could be. Tall and strong and bearded and American. A new sort of man. Who wouldn't love that? Look at the pictures." He handed her the paperback he'd bought his freshman year. "You can't tell me you're not in love with the guy in this photo."

Anastasia snorted. "Yeah. I'm not much into sasquatch."

"Ignore the beard. Just look in his eyes."

Anastasia held the book to her face a while and just looked. "Okay. You're right. Those are great eyes. He could have an eyeball battle with Julie. But, E, great eyes a solid argument for Whitman-is-Dracula do not make."

"Sure, but, wow." Emory took the book back and looked into the one face he knew better than his own. "You might say he's got Alec Baldwin eyes. Just—you just want to fall into them."

"I cannot believe you're still holding that viewing of *Red October* against me."

"You practically pissed yourself, Nastia."

"Emory. You know *nothing* about female anatomy."

Emory held up his hands in surrender.

In their peripheral, Julie moved her feet to the floor in a supple feline motion that arrested their attention. She stood and stretched and Emory wondered, if one of them touched her, she would purr. Julie smiled with a bright genuineness he immediately believed, and showed her adonises out the door. Holy crap they were perfect. Yet as she closed the door behind them and their image lingered on Emory's retinas, she seemed to forget them immediately. She walked over to Emory and Anastasia and elegantly plopped to the floor beside them. "Hi, I'm Julie. We've never been introduced, but you're Emory, right?" He nodded and stupidly held out a hand which she shook. "Nice to meet you. You were talking about Whitman, right? My only real experience was with the body electric in high school, but the teacher made me love it. You study him?"

Emory nodded again.

"I've tried reading him since, but the length of those lines intimidates me. I tend to stick with Emily Dickinson for my 19th-century poetical revolutionaries. What attracted you to him?" She smiled and touched his knee. Instinctively, he wondered, or was it calculated?

He cocked an eyebrow at Anastasia, and said, "I feel like Emerson, maybe. Emerson read *Leaves of Grass* and said, holy crap! Someone's doing it! Someone's becoming new and real and American! And he's *still* the preeminent American man in every way: his costume manly and free, his face sunburnt and bearded, his posture strong and erect, his voice bringing hope! He flings his arms, drawing us with undeniable love to his close embrace! All else seems to burn up under his fierce affection for persons!"

Anastasia tapped his head with her book. "Who said that?"

Emory blushed. "Walt did. In an anonymous review of his own work. He could be a little cocky. But he wasn't wrong." That last sentence came out more vehemently than he'd intended, so he added, "I guess."

"No, it's cool," said Julie. "What could be more American than being cocky? It's cool how much you love him. You don't get to see people being passionate very often. People are so guarded."

"You're right," said Emory. "You are *so* right! Why can't we just be honest about our passions? That's why. . . ." The silence held, and he looked down.

"Why what?" said Julie, softly.

"It's silly. I was going to say that's why lately I've gone online as Bram Stoker. It's not because of vampires—sorry, Anastasia—it's because of how passionate he was. He wrote crazy fanboy letters to Walt Whitman even though he didn't always mail them. He changed his whole life around to work for an actor he loved. And you know what? I can't say much about the actor, but Walt was worthy of the attention. He wrote back. He invited Stoker over. He made him feel loved and important. Even though by this point he was old and not in his best health, he was a good host to a nobody fanboy. Who does that today? Who's *ever* done that? Walt Whitman's done that. And maybe Jesus or Socrates or Mother Teresa or something. Ghandi. But mostly, we're talking about Walt Whitman. He had an amazing soul."

"It sounds like it. Although," she added with a quick grin, "I'm pretty sure Socrates never wrote back. Wasn't he aggressively illiterate?"

Anastasia laughed. "Jesus too, best we know."

"He read in the synagogue," said Julie, "but did he write letters? I don't think so. Mother Teresa, though. I know she wrote that French Mormon woman back."

Julie's gaze moved across the wall and out the front window. Emory glanced but couldn't see anything other than a few branches before a streetlight. "But Whitman must have dealt with nobodies all the time." She turned back to Emory. "Stoker hadn't written *Dracula* yet?"

"No. He was just another protostalker."

Julie nodded. "You know—maybe he liked how pure Stoker's intentions were. Maybe he was sick of people showing off how great they were, trying to be worthy of him."

"You're rorschaching," muttered Anastasia.

Emory shrugged. "Honestly, I haven't read that many letters *to* Whitman. I will say Emerson didn't care for *his* sycophants much. Whitman admired Emerson about as much as Stoker admired Whitman, and Walt really got on Emerson's nerves."

"I guess it's lucky you prefer Walt to Ralph," said Anastasia and spun her book in her hand.

"Yes . . ." trailed Julie, then she returned her eyes to Emory's face. "How did he take it?"

"Who take what?"

"Whitman. How did he feel about being pushed away by Emerson?"

Emory frowned. "Mm. Well. I think he knew publishing Emerson's letter to him without permission was a sketchy thing to do."

Julie laughed and leaned back on her hands—perhaps to give interested (though absent) parties a better view of her bags of fat? Emory wasn't sure if he should wish she had an appropriate audience or be relieved she didn't.

"So you've read Whitman—all of him, I guess?"

"No, I'm always finding something new. I'm not sure I've even read everything in the library yet. So many different versions of the same things. He's hard to keep track of."

"Yeah. So." Julie waved a hand and pursed her lips. "Were they right back then? By our standards, is he 'obscene'?"

"You mean was he gay?"

"Mm, well, that too, I suppose." Julie shrugged. "I thought that was established?"

"Well, yes, maybe, but, I guess— Just because he's *gay* doesn't mean—I mean—gay is not a nineteenth-century term. Thus it's not even possible for Whitman to have been 'gay.' And besides, Whitman worked hard to avoid getting stuck with labels. Who am I to slap a reductive 2005 one on him? No question he would reject it. He was *humanity.* That's his whole *thing.*" Emory waved his hands in the air, then slumped his shoulders and started muttering. "Besides, are gay and straight even things? Shouldn't we all, I don't know, admit to being on some sort of continuum or something? The nineteenth century certainly didn't buy the dichotomy we're forcing people into now. Shouldn't I be able to say those were some handsome guys you had over? I mean, I think?" Emory looked at Anastasia who was graciously trying neither to ignore him nor look at him.

"You think so?"

This new voice, though nearly silent, arrested Emory entirely. He was frozen a moment, then turned to see a slight girl sitting on the couch who reminded him he had once again been treating white as the default human color and he needed to repent.

"Hey, Jilly," said Julie. "How are you always so quiet?"

Emory cleared his throat and said something probably racist. "I've never met anyone named Jilly before."

"My name's Jill." She didn't make eye contact with him. Or her roommates. "My mom wanted me to have a normal white name for resumes. But people call me Jilly. I guess because I'm little."

"You're not so little," Emory said, then regretted.

Anastasia gave her eyes a dramatic roll. "Don't let her fool you, Emory. She introduced herself as Jilly. She walked in and I said, 'I'm Anastasia,' then Julie said, 'Hi, I'm Julie,' then Jilly said, 'Hi, I'm Jilly.' It was kind of funny for some reason and we all laughed, like the end of an old sitcom. Happiest day of my life. Don't take that away from me, Jilly."

Jilly shrugged. "Jilly's fine."

Emory wondered at Jilly/Jill's downturned face and said, "It's nice to meet you, Jill. What were you saying?"

"What you said about—about a continuum."

"Sure, I mean—people require love. Right?"

"Sure." Jilly's voice, already small, all but disappeared. Emory felt he was feeling her words in the hairs on his arm—or that her voice was telepathic.

"So—thought experiment." Emory smiled. He'd been wanting to try this one out. "Imagine all the men in the world die tomorrow. Poof. It's a, I don't know, a masculine rapture."

Anastasia barked a laugh. "I'll sign that petition."

"'Masculine rapture.' Whitman could've used that," offered Julie.

"I would buy that band's album," Anastasia said.

Emory shrugged. "Anyway, you think all you fine, feminine, heterosexual-but-manless ladies will spend the next fifty years without a special someone? No way."

"I never thought of that," said Julie.

"I think about it all the time," said Anastasia. "Freaking boys." She paused, then held her hands out, reading an invisible marquee. *Freaking Boys & the Masculine Rapture. Opening this July on Broadway."*

Emory pushed her knee. "Very nice, Anastasia. I'll give you co-author credit."

"That's what I like about you, Emory. Your generosity." She stuck out her tongue.

"So," said Jilly, pausing until Anastasia's tongue disappeared. "No one's straight or gay?"

"Your mileage may vary, but that's basically what Kinsey preached, right?"

"It makes sense." Jilly pulled her feet up under her thin, almost twelve-year-old frame.

Emory pointed a shoulder in Jilly's direction. "Are you comfortable?"

Jilly looked at him. "What do you mean?"

"Just looks like your typical student apartment couch, no firmness left or anything."

Anastasia pointed a finger and waved it at each of them. "All together now: 'That's what she said.'"

Julie groaned. "C'mon, Anastasia. At least be classy enough to say, 'Said the choirgirl to the bishop.'"

A high-pitched, muffled giggle interrupted them and all three heads turned to see Jilly covering her face with her hands.

Julie turned back to Emory. "So—are you taking a class on Whitman or something?

"I'm doing my master's thesis on him."

Julie clapped her hands. "Ladies, we have a postgrad in our midst."

Anastasia glumphed. "You see me sitting here, right?"

Julie slapped the floor. "Two postgrads in our midst! Tell us more, Emory. We already know all the basics about Sanskrit."

Emory wobbled his head a bit. "Well, it's reception studies, obviously. Creative thesis. Right now I'm experimenting with writing personal letters to Walt from me—à la Bram Stoker—and then writing his responses in Whitmanesque verse."

"Cool," said Julie.

"Not really," said Anastasia. "Sorry, that sounded unkind. What I mean is he's doing as much research as anyone, but unless you know the field as well as he does, it won't show."

Jilly raised her hand. "What do you mean, it won't show?"

Emory was about to answer, but Anastasia kicked him.

"Hey."

"Hush." Anastasia dogeared a page and set her novel down. "He does all this research, but because his thesis is creative, all that research is evident only in its invisible-ness—it's all embedded in the letters and poetry. Whitman would never say directly that he was gay-not-gay, but it has to show in what Emory writes. Obliquely. Not easy. And you need to convince a bunch of half-interested people in something they can't be bothered to look for."

"I'll have a seventy-page introduction, remember."

"No one wants to read that crap, Emory."

"*They* will read that crap. It's you who doesn't want to read it, Nastia."

"And I am no one."

"Don't say that."

They all turned to look at Jilly. She shrugged.

Julie looked at Jilly longer than was strictly necessary, thought Emory, but then her attention returned to him bringing its weird mix of sadness and surprise. "So, you write the letters as yourself."

"Yeah, but the letters always get way too personal. I can't put that stuff up for review."

Julie raised an eyebrow. "WWWWD?"

Emory blinked. "What?"

Anastasia laughed at him. "You can do it."

"Oh. Got it."

Emory looked at Anastasia who was back in her book. Anastasia glanced over at him. "I'm being a jerk, aren't I? Sorry. And that mea culpa sounds sarcastic, doesn't it? I'm sorry. Still sounding sarcastic. Guess I'm just a bitch. That's all there is to it."

Emory shrugged. "The world needs bitches."

Jilly giggled again, then cleared her throat.

Anastasia nodded. "Being a bitch is a highly useful skill and an integral part of my self-identity. You should all consider adding bitch to your toolbag. My own problem's turning it off and on." She grabbed an empty gum wrapper from the carpet to use as a bookmark, then dropped the book to the floor and pushed back into her chair. "Tell us, oh itinerant preacher, what would Walt Whitman do?"

Emory cleared his throat. "He would, um, embrace his inner, you know."

"His inner bitch. Exactly. Octuple-you-dee. Just like Julie said."

Jilly leaned over onto the couch's arm and propped her chin on the backs of her hands. "What did Walt Whitman do about his straight admirer?"

Emory waved a hand. "Stoker? Not much. They only met a couple times. He did leave him his lecture notes on Lincoln though, kind of interesting." Silence descended, so Emory pulled out his next chestnut. "You want to hear about Stoker and Oscar Wilde?"

"Oh *my* yes," said Anastasia, sounding only about 60 percent sarcastic, he decided.

"So Wilde had a huge crush on this woman—"

Anastasia was scandalized. "What? But Wilde was totally gay!"

Emory sighed. "You haven't been hearing me. Wilde was married, you know. And he also had a crush on this woman. But Stoker married her and it took years before Wilde would talk to him again."

Anastasia's scandalized face grew more delicious. "Shut up. That's crazy."

Julie shook her head. "No. . . . I don't think so. Why can't anyone love anyone? I'm not talking about sexuality, though. I'm talking about . . . Christianity, maybe? I don't know if crush equals charity but—they are similar, right? I mean, except for the occasional sociopath, people are kind to those who crush on them. Or at least they try to ignore them in a loving sort of way. So maybe—shouldn't we be able to love everyone we meet? Maybe even each person deeply? If only for a moment. Flashes of the Christ mind. That's—beautiful."

Anastasia shuddered. "Well, I'm still too much the bitch to cop *that* b-word. Also, I don't think you understand crushes. Crushes are inherently selfish."

Julie cocked her head. "How do you mean?"

"Think about it. Crushes involve one person only. The object of a crush isn't a person; it's an idealized, imagined thing. You have to move past the crush before the object becomes a person."

"Semantics."

"Back me up, Emory."

"I don't know. Crushes seem more liminal than selfish to me."

"Jilly?"

She shrugged and leaned back. "I get what you're saying, but if I agree with you, I'll feel guilty."

Emory pointed at Jilly. "There. That's the problem."

"What."

"Crushes are, perhaps, like you say, objectifying in some sense, but you can't know if another human will love you back. Think about a painting or a sculpture or a movie—those things *can't* love you back. That doesn't make me selfish for loving *Eternal Sunshine*."

Julie closed her eyes. "So you're okay with treating people like aesthetic experiences."

"I'm not a physicist. Does observing someone change them?"

"Yes," said Julie and Jilly at the same time.

"But not for the same reason," said Jilly. Emory thought it best not to ask what she meant. Instead, he watched Anastasia look at her.

Anastasia stood. "Okay, I'm brushing my teeth and heading to bed."

Julie grabbed her pantleg as Anastasia stood. "It's only ten."

"I know. Bitch gotta sleep." She patted Julie's head and walked off.

Jilly watched Anastasia go then stood. "I'll—I'll go brush too. It was nice to meet you."

"Thanks."

Silence. The sound of items moving around in a bathroom. Mumbles. Something falling to the floor.

Emory looked over at Julie who was staring into the space abandoned by Jilly's departure. Her brow was slightly furrowed.

"Sixteen cents for your thoughts?"

Julie started and looked at him. "You think my thoughts are sixteen times more valuable than the going rate?"

He shrugged. "I've found it gets more of a response than 'Oh, nothing.'"

"Way to hack the thought economy. I'm—just thinking about Jilly."

"May I ask?"

She shook her head. "I think roommate confidentiality comes into play. Especially since my thoughts are purely speculative."

"Mm."

"What about your roommates? You must have some."

"Yes, but my apartment's clear on the north side of campus. Draftwood? Do you know it?"

"No. I've kind of stopped traveling."

"Well. You don't need to." Emory started putting his books back in his bag. "You know, Julie. I like what you said about crushes being tiny pieces of Christ's love. She's not my roommate, so confidentiality does not apply, but Anastasia first invited me over to watch boys fall in love with you—and I think I know that moment you're talking about. I've seen men lock onto you." He looked at her for a moment, waited for her to nod. "I don't suppose I should anticipate loving anyone longer than that. So finding beauty in those moments— You make it sound noble."

Julie held up her hand to stop him. "Thanks, Emory, but back up. What?"

"What what?"

"Anastasia asked you over to watch boys fall in love with me?"

"Yeah. I'm sorry. I shouldn't have— I mean—" Emory set

his bag aside again. "How do you feel about that?"

Julie rearranged herself to better see him. "I don't know. It's annoying but. But I can't pretend I don't know what she's talking about. Does that make me full of myself?"

"No. It's obviously true, so no."

Julie leaned forward again and fixed his eyes with hers. "Something that drives me crazy is how people around here—or maybe it's people our age—or maybe it's a Mormon thing—feel those momentary flashes of connection and immediately project them into eternity. Why do moments need to be that big? I feel connected to you right now. Doesn't mean we should shop for rings. I'm not capable of seeing eternity at 10pm, sitting on our ugly carpet in Provo, Utah. Redshift moves eternity right off the visible spectrum."

"I have no idea what that means."

Julie buried her face between her knees for a moment, then reattached herself to his eyes. "Sorry. Physics joke. Or physics metaphor. Something."

They sat and listened to spitting and the water turning off and on in the pipes until Julie asked, "Do you think Wilde was genuinely mad at him?"

Emory shrugged. "'Mad'? At Stoker? At first, I guess. Anger doesn't last, though. It requires too much energy. Bitterness, though. I don't know. Stoker married her so Wilde's chance was gone forever. I still remember lost opportunities. Don't you?"

Julie didn't answer.

Emory leaned back on his hands and looked up at the ceiling. "My art teacher in high school used to say you can be anything you want in life. But not everything."

Julie pursed her lips.

"So that's when I dropped art. I picked literature. Choice made. But, when I think about it, I feel a hole where that potential, that possibility, died. Where that path's gate shut behind me."

Julie smiled. "That's poetry, Emory. I guess you chose right."

"Did I? Maybe I could've done both? Who knows. But bed is made, let me lie," and, in emphasis, he lay on the carpet.

Julie turned herself to see him better. "Do you think careers are like people then?"

Emory turned his head to her. "How do you mean?"

"Anyone is possible, but not everyone."

Emory looked back at the ceiling. ". . . No. For some of us . . . I'm not sure even *any*one is possible."

"What do you mean?"

"Nothing." He could feel her looking at him so turned his head away. "I don't know."

Julie reached out and lightly rested her fingers on his shoulder. "Here's what I know. You're cute. You're a desirable number of inches tall. You're a poet. You feel things deeply. You're easy to be around. I mean—we haven't really talked before, but you don't seem boring. I can certainly imagine *you*, as we sit here, right now. Most people—especially men—I tire of in . . . much too short a time. I'm not that charitable, inherently. No, it's true. But you? You have this thing—I want to say injury?—this *vulnerability*—I want to hold you—metaphorically, of course—to heal you. Given the chance, I think anyone could feel the same. I think that might be what girls want." She sighed. "I'm not sure. I look around, but I'm not sure."

She scooted forward and used her hand to turn his face to her. "No pressure. But, you know, you, kind of, seem like you need— Here. Let me kiss you."

Emory propped himself on his elbows and looked into her face. It was open and holy and pure and he had no interest. "That's for princesses." He sat up and took her hands. "Look. If I could love a girl, Julie, I could love you. You're as perfect as Nastia claimed. And cool to boot. How could anyone *not* love you?"

"But you don't." She swallowed a sound—a laugh? "I wish I wasn't so excited by your disinterest." She squeezed his hands. "It's a sure way to get my attention."

"I'm gay, Julie. I'm gay."

"You— But what you said about continua?"

Emory's eyes bored into hers. "I have to believe that's true. And I have had little crushes on girls. Sort of. I mean, if Oscar Wilde can, I can, right? So there must be a continuum. And I can still hope. Of course, I'll still be alone."

"You can be anything you want to be. . . ." She closed her eyes, so he looked at her lids.

"So I hear."

The rest of the apartment had gone quiet. A car drove past Brick House. Julie looked back up. "What about . . . men?"

Emory shook his head. "I'm just keeping my heart locked up. The less I open it, the safer I stay. You can't be hurt by the fall if you stay off the highwire. If you stay in the garden. If you mix your metaphors."

Julie attempted a nod. "Locked up. I guess so. I'm not really one to talk. All I ever do is hurt people. I've wondered if being gay—further along that continuum—would be easier."

Emory laughed without meaning it. "Sorry to disappoint."

"It's all right. I do it to people all the time." She made a flickery movement with her fingers, as if she were manipulating two pairs of chopsticks. "Even myself."

"Even yourself?"

Julie shrugged. "Julie the inspirational speaker tells herself if you're not disappointed in yourself you don't comprehend your potential. But I don't mean it in a cocky way."

"I didn't think that of you."

She smiled. "You're a nice guy, Emory."

"It's gotten me this far."

"Yeah. Anyway, what I meant was, it seems the advantage of being gay is you lose the communication barrier between the sexes. That's a positive, right?"

Emory looked at her a moment before breaking into loud laughter. "Oh my gosh, Julie. You have *no* idea. You should see the politics and soap opera and and and gossip and disaster that's always floating through my gay friends. I tell them I'm straight. They know otherwise, but they let me pretend. So I just watch and think maybe I'm lucky, having locked myself on the outside. I'll just keep writing my letters—prayers, almost—to my gay Jesus knowing that he—or at least my fictional construction of him—understands me and forgives me and accepts me."

"What about the real Jesus?" Julie covered her mouth, as if trying to hide the question's source. "Sorry."

Emory shook his head. "It's okay. I'm a good Mormon boy. I have Jesus too. But Walt's kind of like . . . a bodhisattva between me and messiah. He's my Virgin Mary. My Saint Sebastian. I'm not ready for a god's full glory."

Julie's face broke. "Oh, Emory." She took his hand. "Are you happy?"

"Hhhhh. Happy enough. Now and then. I don't know. I will be, right? I take the sacrament. This is all part of that great plan of happiness. So . . . sure. I can be anything I want to be. I want to be happy. Ergo, I shall be." He shrugged. "I just have to figure stuff out. Me. I just have to figure me out."

He lifted his eyes again; Julie took them and held them as she moved over to hug him, to hold him until he held her back. There they sat, arms around, not knowing quite what the other was feeling. As for Emory, he imagined Julie as God the Mother, removing his solitude more permanently than his own mother could, if only for a single crushlike moment. Emory felt a tear slip down his face and wondered how long it had been since they'd moved. "I should go."

"Okay." But she didn't let go. He felt her breathe.

"I have a letter to write. Maybe a response too. Maybe the response first. I don't know."

"Okay."

She pushed softly away.

"My mother—" Emory sniffed and wiped his nose on his wrist. "My mother told me I would come to BYU and meet a girl who would save me. I always thought she meant make me straight—and I always thought she would be wrong. But maybe she was right. Not about making me straight, but about saving me."

Julie shook her head, looked down. "No. I'm just a girl, Emory. I can't change anyone. Not even myself."

He exhaled. "I feel different. Ineffable but different."

"Not ineffably happy?"

He made a sound like a laugh. "If it's happiness, it's definitely ineffable. And it won't last." He touched his face. "I guess I just feel good having been straight—I mean—*honest* with you. Anyway. Don't sell yourself short, Julie. I don't know what I'm talking about, so don't worry yourself figuring it out. Just: thank you. We had a moment. Add it to your collection. It'll refract sunlight a bit differently than the others."

She grunted and smiled. "Whatever. Take it up with Walt Whitman."

Emory smiled back. "I will."

She reclined on her elbows. "And, just so you know, I don't think it matters if I'm a boy or a girl. I don't think it matters if *you're* a boy or a girl. I don't think it matters if God's a boy or a girl. What matters is we share hugs that look cheesy to outsiders. That we're alike in the household of faith. All that crap."

Emory slapped his backpack and nodded. "All that crap. All that holy crap."

Julie stood and helped him up. "Come over and read us some of the poetry Whitman's writing back to you. I can tell already I'll like it better than the original."

"You'd better not."

She hugged him again and let him out.

Emory stood a moment on the front porch and looked into the black sky. He couldn't read the stars, but he could tell there were constellations to be seen. He tried to connect some dots from one to two to three, but nothing made sense. Not yet. But he could see the stars and he took on faith that the constellations were there.

Meet Hathor

Yemalla!

My ancestors lived on the west coast of Africa and were stolen further west to America. My great-grandparents left America's south coast and traveled to her west coast to build ships to defend her. My mother raised me a few cities south of those shipyards. I never knew my father, but my mother discovered our Father and we both were baptized Saints.

Yemalla!

When I was twelve my mother became what one social worker called a lunatic—no offense, Yemalla—and I was swept up by a sweet family in my ward, a family as white as the bread they were too moneyed to buy, who cared for me and gave me the gift of endless Internet where I learned that once people of my skin could not fully be Saints, where I learned my Mormon family has a Mother but cannot speak her name, where I learned my African ancestors had a Mother and your name is Yemalla.

Upon discovering the trapdoor in the closet of the room she shared with Anastasia, Jill had arrayed her clothing to hide it. She had surreptitiously stacked boxes to make a ladder, then arranged some bedding abandoned by previous housemates to make herself a beanbag-chair-esque nest in her secret attic. She could walk beam-to-beam like stepping over civilizations. She could peek through vents into every room of the house (though some rooms' sovereignty she accepted). She could be everywhere and nowhere. She could know what everyone said. She could descend and join a conversation if she wished, or she could just Jane Goodall this strange species she lived with. She could observe and practice love as does Yemalla, the ocean, the moon, the mother of spirits, the protector of children.

And come night, she might sit before the great window and prop herself up with blankets and pillows and watch the stars and, when visible, the moon. And when she saw the moon mother, her heart would sing.

Yemalla!

Others called you Gleti, the mother of all stars! And just as thy children differ from one another in brightness and glory, so am I less bright and glorious than—you know. But I've kept my promise, Mother. I've not watched her—or any of my roommates—in moments of undress or intimacy. I've been good. I have. I promise.

I believe what I've been told, Yemalla. I believe in Jesus, my brother, your son; I believe in his father, your lover. But they tell me I shouldn't pray to my mother. And so I talk, only talk. I talk only to you. Forgive me, but I cannot pray to a father.

And I get what this means without therapy.

Yemalla!

I am alone. I am surrounded by beauty and kindness. Everyone sees me and sees difference, but not how much, nor what it means—they're too polite to see so much.

The Egyptians also had a moon goddess. Before leaving Montana for Provo, Jill took a flight home to Oakland to walk the old streets and to have Hathor's hieroglyph tattooed on her chest low enough that no tshirt would ever reveal it, a square with a falcon inside, standing tall and regal. An inkjet copy of Hathor with her cow horns and sundisk headdress—red overalls-like dress with her breasts hanging out, the dress clinging tight to her slim stomach and legs and around her backside—she kept taped to the inside of her Bible as a reminder in church and religion classes that the Mother was in here, somewhere, and Jill just had to keep looking. Was she Ashtoreth? If so, why were the Father's prophets so bitter toward her?

Where is she?

Yemalla!

Last night—she—spoke with one of Anastasia's friends. He confided in her that he was gay and she did not push him away or mock him as would have been reasonable for him to expect in this valley where differences, in the name of Zion, must be comfortably invisible. I know I repeat myself, Yemalla, but remember: I have said she's special. She is open and she loves. Perhaps she would say to me, too, what you do not?

Yemalla!

The Egyptians called you Mistress of the West and taught that you welcome the dead into their next life. If I knew that were true, I would consider death worthy fare. But I don't want to wait that long. I want to hear from you now. But who speaks for you? I have listened in meetings and conferences and I have not heard your voice. Could she? Can she? Can you give her the words I need to hear?

Yemalla!

I have ears to hear!

Make her my "bodhisattva" too!

O, Hathor, personification of feminine love and joy and motherhood—I want to be like you. Not to be mother of all the saints and stars, but a mother. But I am small, still a child, eternally a child, invisible, black in a sea of white, alone, forgotten, and who here could make me a mother? That path is closed to me.

Yemalla!

This friend said that we are all along a continuum between fully one thing and fully another, but that seems . . . too simple. A line insufficient to cover this territory. We're more like . . . a cube. A space. And maybe I'm not in her corner, but I am far from the opposite corner, far even from the center. And mothers do not live where I live.

Did you greet my mother when she died?

Did you bring her to herself? Did you remind her of me?

Jill's mother had named her Jill Luther King—a name, she said, that would prove suitably white while maintaining a powerful black respectability. But even ignoring her middle name and saying simply her name was "Jill King" led to the necessary hope and disappointment of white and black alike when Jill was forced to say, No. No, I am not related to Reverend King.

She always referred to him as "Reverend King." No one asked her why. She had never asked herself why.

And everyone referred to her as Jilly.

When they referred to her at all.

Yemalla!

Only through a conscious effort of will during her freshman year of college had Jill finally been able to stop referring to herself, to this slight black girl, as Jilly. And then she moved off campus with its promise of reinvention, only to discover she would live with the girl who had sat ten seats down from her in the BIO 100 auditorium.

"Hi, I'm Julie."

"Hi, I'm Jilly."

Such a small thing, to sound like her, but for a moment.

But!

Yemalla!

Yes, she's kind to me—she's kind to everyone—she's even kind to the worst of boys, after they've left, when Maddysyn and Ashleigha begin to tear them apart—

"And Jake. Real people aren't named Jake. And his nose! What, was it broken?"

"I know, right?"

But Julie shakes her head slowly. "It suggests character. He has stories. He has a background."

"And he does that weird thing with his voice!"

"Where it sounds like he's hiccupping."

"And he talks about guns all the time."

"And that creepy thing he said about the Columbine guys—"

"—using the wrong guns—"

"—and picking the wrong day—"

Julie paused. "He—" She paused again. "—has so much empathy, even for the villains."

But, on the other hand, even of the kindest, dearest, sweetest, cutest, kindest boys she grows tired, disappearing into her room to crank out a page essay on toddler nutrition or to do the math in some thirty-year-old textbook she picked up at a thrift store.

Yes, yes, yes. I watch her. I've seen her avoid the good and kiss a fool bound for disaster. And I wonder. And I hope.

Why doesn't she pick one? She could take whichever she wants—she dates ten times a week—but never with the same boy twice—and I—

Yemalla!

Thanks to science, I know you don't shine your own light, that you just reflect the sun—as you, as Hathor, wore a sundisk on your head. But your children, the stars, they shine on their own. Am I like you? Content to reflect? Or am I your child—and shine?

Is that what motherhood is? Reflection?

But the sun shines by burning itself up. Endless, constant destruction.

I want to create.

But creation and reflection—they can't be the same thing, can they?

Yemalla!

I could be happy reflecting her. But she cannot make me a mother.

Two weeks ago. Julie sits at the kitchen table with her textbook on childhood nutrition. From the living room she can hear the *twins trying to distract three boys—Charlie, Charles, Ross—from their quest, who is sitting in the kitchen trying to focus on ribo-flavin and niacin and the developmental importance of these and other B vitamins.*

From above, like an off-duty Gabriel, Jill watches her. In the margins of her books, Julie tries to express the relationship between vitamins and growth as a mathematical function, but keeps scribbling them out until she throws her pen down and her head back—for a moment Jill fears she has been spotted—and says, "What's wrong with them? Other than their names, I mean? All nice and attractive enough. Decent . . . prospects.

"Utterly boring."

Was it a prayer? Thinking aloud? Jill gazes invisibly into Julie's eyes. Then Julie sighs and slams her book shut and leaves the room.

Jill hears the boys' voices jump half an octave and increase in speed and intensity and volume and aggression. And she walks back to her home by the window.

Yemalla!

If someone beautiful and beloved can be alone, what hope have I? Especially here, in a white church, a straight church, and me—a ratchetty little Oaktown girl. What am I doing here?

Jill has tried many means of getting closer to the moon. In late fall however—or in Provo, ever—anything involving being outside or naked is out. She holds out her hand to hold a moonbeam as doors open and close downstairs.

Yemalla!

I don't wish to be alone. But I can't ask for love and I can't receive it. She speaks of marriage and is surrounded by suitors. But I watch her. She only relaxes away from them. She's only happy when she's alone. And if that's the case—

I don't want to be alone, Yemalla. Mother. Mom.

I don't want to be alone.

A crashing sound startles Jill and she rushes to the kitchen, stumbling once.

"Holy crap," *says Ashleigha.* "Did you hear that? What was that? Raccoons?"

Julie is sitting on the kitchen table holding her elbow, swaying forwards and backwards, and biting her lip.

"Because if it is raccoons, they've got to get them out. My dad said raccoons carry a disease in their poop? It's pretty bad. We could all die. There it is again!"

Jill slips down to her closet and bursts out, eliciting a quick scream from Anastasia. She runs to the kitchen and pops open the freezer, pulling out a bag of corn. "Here."

Julie takes it and holds it to her elbow. "Thanks, Jilly. How did you know?"

But Jill is already picking up the three books, two cookie sheets, and broken glass that are scattered about the floor.

Ashleigha keeps rattling on about the dangers of raccoons and how not funny that raccoon scene in Elf was because in real life Will Ferrell would have died. "I'm going to call the landlord and demand he get the raccoons out tonight."

"We don't have raccoons."

Ashleigha doesn't realize Jilly has spoken, so she says "What?" *to Julie.*

"She said we don't have raccoons."

Ashleigha rolls her eyes. "I'm from Utah. They probably don't *even have raccoons in Oakland or wherever."*

"Yes we do." Jilly dumps a handful of glass onto a cookie sheet. "They live in the sewers."

"Gross."

"Thank you, Jilly." Julie leans back a bit and exhales. "Wow that hurt."

Jilly chances looking into Julie's face. "What happened?"

Julie shakes her head and blushes. "Nothing. We were just moving stuff around and I elbowed the table. Nothing fancy."

"Are you okay?"

Ashleigha mumbles something about picking up Maddysyn from campus and storms out of the kitchen.

"Why is she so mad?" Jill glances briefly at Julie and sees her neck turning to watch Ashleigha go.

"I don't know. It was my cup. But I suppose she's the one who invited Charlie over. And I'm the one he asked out."

"Did you say yes?"

"Not exactly. I'm tired of boys making it hard between the twins and me."

"It's not your fault," Jill says, silently adding, you're beautiful and kind and charming and everyone loves you.

"It kind of is," says Julie, and hops off the table to return the corn to the freezer. "Thanks for letting me use that."

"Sure."

"Let me grab the broom."

Jill sets the other cookie sheet and the books on the table and dumps the glass into the trash. Then she steps just outside the kitchen—first checking her shoes for glass—and watches Julie sweep, who brings her elegance even to that task, her arms follow-

ing perfect parabolas through the air as the broom gathers dust
and shards from linoleum. She's a sort of perfect Jill's never been
so close to before, not for so long, not with months left in the year.

"How do you do it, Julie?"

Julie remains in dance with the broom. "Do what?"

"You just— You have a way about you that people are attracted to. But you don't have room for that many people. So how do
you—decide?"

Julie stops sweeping at this, her hands atop the broom and under her chin. "This isn't a problem unique to me. Everyone attracts
more people than they have room for."

"No."

"Like the inn in Bethlehem. The trick is—how do we know who
to turn away. How do you choose, Jilly?"

"I don't know." She leans against the jamb. "I've never really
had to."

"Sure you have. After, you know, your mom, all those people in
your ward offered to take you in—how did you choose?"

"I—how did you know about that?"

Julie smiles and returns to sweeping. "You told me. I listened."

"I—I did?"

"Well. Sort of. I was sitting on the porch and you were lying on
the roof—how did you get up there?—and I heard bits. I'm sorry.
I wasn't trying to eavesdrop. At first, I thought I heard my name,
that you were talking to me."

"You heard me—? Oh my go—!" Jilly's eyes drop to the floor and
her face burns hot. Julie leans the broom against the fridge and
runs over to her. "Oh, Jilly, Jilly. I'm sorry. I wasn't trying to spy. I
promise. All I know is there were three families—"

Jilly finds herself hugged by Julie and clutches her back, trying to hide her sudden occasional sobs while knowing that holding Julie assures she will feel each one.

"I'm sorry, Jilly. I'm so so sorry."

"No. No, it's okay." *She took a deep breath and pushed herself far enough away to look up into Julie's eyes, while still holding onto her upper arms.* "I'm Jill."

"Jill?"

"Jilly . . . is silly. I'm . . . not."

"Fair enough. Jill."

"One family meant well but was already on welfare. One family was just proving how good they were. That left the Meads. Who were perfect anyway. They loved me.

"How could they not?"

Jill has never looked this long at Julie before. She feels a bit dizzy and holds on tighter. "You mean—?"

Julie shrugs and sits Jill in a chair. She returns to sweeping, the broom waltzing under the table, once brushing Jill's shoe. "I don't see you that often; we don't talk so much. But I feel I know you all the same. If I were in pain, I could come to you. If I had a secret, you would keep it. If I were alone, you would sit with me. N'est-ce pas?"

"Oui."

"And I would do the same for you. No matter how many boys are lounging in the front room, stinking it up with their naked ambitions, I would sit with you."

"Even if—" *Jill feels herself disappearing into the hallway, the shadows sucking her in.*

"Even if even-ifs."

"Even if—I'm apostate?"

Julie stops sweeping again and with her eyes pulls Jill back from her darkness. "Even if." She holds a hand, palm upward, to Jill, a metaphor. "And how are you apostate?"

"I—" Jill listens to as much of the house as she can from where she sits. Then she whispers, "I can't—can't—focus my faith on anyone but—Heavenly Mother. I, you know, believe in God the Eternal Father and in His Son Jesus Christ and in the Holy Ghost—but I believe in Her more."

Julie props the broom against a wall and pulls a chair beside Jill's and sits. She reaches into Jill's lap and takes her hands. "I don't think that's a sin."

"Do you—?"

"I don't know. I don't think about her much. But when I do, I don't see how I can ever think of anyone else."

"Yes."

Julie's hands are warm and soft—and dry as the broom handle. They do not emit the line of electricity Jill expected. Instead, they seem more to draw from Jill her tightness and solitude.

"Julie?"

"Mm?"

"How do you know when—someone—is right—or not right for you?"

"Pff. I don't. I'm not the person to talk to."

"But you tell the twins—all the time—that you'll be married before you graduate."

"Yeah." Julie's eyes drift to the sink. Jill's eyes follow and together they watch a drop reach enough mass to fall from the faucet. "That's what I want."

"Do you?"

"Why else would I come to BYU?"

Jill looks away and surprises herself by saying, "I will never be a mother."

Julie had been leaning forward to stand, but now she falls back into her chair. "Sure you will."

"No."

Julie reaches forward and tips up Jill's face. "How can you be so sure?"

"I'm . . . not made for men."

"You have—" Julie makes a gesture at her own body. "You have all this, the same as anyone."

"Hardware with no software." Not an analogy Jill has ever thought of before, but she can read its accuracy upon Julie's face as it passes through layers of clarity and uncertainty and emotions Jill does not wish defined.

They sit in silence. Jill thinks she hears pages turning as Anastasia walks into the bathroom and begins her ablutions.

Julie looks away first. "I'm not sure what to say."

"I never am."

Julie nods. "Have you always—?"

"Yes. I think."

"You haven't— Not anyone in—?"

"No," lies Jill. "Of course not."

Julie accepts this, but Jill sees she knows otherwise.

"I'm sorry, Julie."

"No. It doesn't change anything."

"You don't need my burdens. You have enough of your own."

Julie slides off her chair and kneels before Jill. "Don't be crazy. My troubles are nothing compared to your troubles. You've lost your mother. Your mother, Jilly! Jill. Sorry."

"It's okay."

"You can lay any burdens on me you want. But I can't— You know."

"I know." But Jill lays her palm against Julie's face anyway—it will be the only time—she knows that. "It's enough." And she stands and escapes out of the kitchen and past Anastasia's bathroom gargling and up the boxes into her attic.

Yemalla!

I didn't mean to—to— I don't know what I did. But—

—even as I sit here, I press my hands together—my hands that just touched hers—and feel something like peace.

Is this my answer?

Will it last?

Is this your message?

Yemalla?

What comes next?

Jill stands at the great window and watches Julie slip down the steps to take the arm of a fuzzy, redheaded kid, his face reflecting the blue of the moon.

Another night, another boy.

Is this her answer?

Yemalla!

Meet The Big Blue Ox

BIG BLUE OX
OPEN HOUSE

come see **BYU** engineering's new
M A R V E L

Friday in the Clyde Building
6pm

Although ostensibly an outreach to nonengineers, as the dark-headed girl was a frequenter of the Clyde building's lobby corkboard she likely knew that these events were really only ever offered to engineers. De facto, that is. She never showed up anyway so she must have known. And everyone else on campus just saw a photo and caption in *The Daily Universe* ex post facto.

Tim knew this as he reached into his mouth and pulled out a bologna ring that had stuck between his molars. He'd seen her before. He knew she kept a socket wrench in her pink backpack that sometimes she would spin between her fingers, but nothing else about her suggested engineering student. And he would know if she were. Girls were a limited resource around here. He had a friend who hung outside the auditorium and watched the Comms 101 class that had mysteriously been scheduled in their building. "Lots of freshman female flesh." And the only reliable source in the entire building.

He gave up on his fingers and pulled the toothpick from his pocketknife. There. Finally. He stuffed the last bit of sandwich in his mouth and, since she was still standing there, decided to talk to her. She was not the sort of girl he usually talked to, but he'd been a missionary. He was used to talking to the weird, the strange, the glamorous. Street contacting in Manhattan, yo.

"Hey." His mouth was still a bit full and his words were muffled. He swallowed and tried again. "Hey."

"Hi."

"You want to come see the Big Blue Ox today?"

"What is it?"

"Ah. Good question." He doublechecked the flier. "I didn't say, did I? Shoot. Oh well. It's like a solar-powered six-wheeled, autonomous pack animal. You know. Like for Indiana Jones, 2005 version."

"Cool. It works?"

"Heck, yes!" She gave him a sisterly sort of smile he found encouraging. "And we're taking it to the Mojave for a competition next week. We got to beat Purdue and Stanford to be happy."

"Rivals?"

"Not exactly. I just have a friend at each school. They're not doing the same kind of engineering and aren't working on their school's projects, but still."

The girl set her head at an angle, a finger working its way up and down her upper arm. It reminded him of those goofy perpetual-motion birds drinking their water.

"It's going to be cool, though. We talked the DI into giving us all the crap people give them that's too busted to sell and we're making a course out of broken-up toys and ripped-up leisure suits and stuff. It's going to be awesome."

"Are you club president?"

"Nah. We only have one because BYUSA insists but I'm not even sure who it is. Not me though. I'm only a junior. Though, considering how long it takes us to graduate, I'm really more like a sophomore. I guess."

The girl nodded and looked past him into what appeared to be "the middle distance."

She was bored, Tim was bored, so he shrugged, said "See ya!" and walked off.

$$\tau = \frac{d\mathbf{L}}{dt} = \frac{d(I\boldsymbol{\omega})}{dt} = I\boldsymbol{\alpha}$$

Tim sat in front of Brother Donaldson's office in an ancient green plastic chair. All he needed was to pick up the key to the empty lab where they were setting up the course, but the door was closed and knocking seemed awful forward. But he'd been here twenty minutes and everyone was waiting with garbage sacks full of who knows what. He stood and held his fist to the door. Soundlessly. Took a step back. Gave his fist a running start. It landed soundlessly again. Interruption was the worst. Then, suddenly, his hand knocked against the door.

"It's open."

Tim proved it so, enough to let in a quarter of his face.

"Tim! You're late! Here. Come grab my keys. Just open it up then bring them back."

Tim finished opening the door and there she was. Amelia McDonald. In a sorta tight pink tshirt and her navy surplus peacoat and her orange jeans and her bun throwing strands of grungy blonde hair into her face, bisecting her eyebrows and cheekbones with reckless romantic abandon. Tim smiled—but it didn't feel like a smile as it lay lopsided on his face—stumbled into the room, nodded jerkily at each, took the keys, and fled.

Amelia McDonald.

Everyone knew she was the best engineer of '07. Even the most chauvinistic pricks in the department didn't knock her and couldn't ignore her. Tim's freshman year, she had won the blindfolded sliderule competition—which had only been a legitimate contest for second place—then gone on a mission where—he'd heard—she'd spent six months traveling around whatever Central American country she was in fixing wells and filtration systems and stuff.

No one asked Tim to fix anything on his mission. He didn't even get a bike to maintain. It was just all subway all the time.

Tim had a hiccup in his step all the way to the lab. Then he sent Paul back with the keys. He couldn't focus on making the track but, when they had finished, it was awesome anyway. An entire hill of Barbie parts? A morass of heavy-metal tshirt remnants? They really should have put posters all over the school. Wonder if it's too late to find someone with a video camera so we can put this online. Somebody must know how to do that. But whatever. The track was great. That's what mattered.

Tim scuffed one scuffed shoe with the other, then ran to the bathroom to pee.

When he returned, the room behind the pilfered police-line tape was still as packed with segregated trash, but the other side was crowded with engineering students and faculty and a handful of others who didn't fit the profile. Tim struggled to keep his gaze straight ahead. Better not to know whether Amelia had come or not. He just squeezed through to the tape and looked out at Jesse and Phil whose legs were sticking out of an ad hoc tent made of stapled-together towel fragments. Then they wiggled out backwards and some sarcastic dope in the crowd whooped like it was sexy. Phil smiled and blushed and waved and pushed his glasses up his nose. Jesse, though, was a showman. He put on some swagger, stepping wide and out and raising his hands and asking for cheers, which he received, after the manner of nerdy Clyde-building residents. Jesse reveled in it for a moment then gestured at Phil who made an *ope!* sound and jumped back into the tent, returning with a megaphone, which he swiftly handed to Jesse.

"HkkkLLkk, kkNGkkNkkkkRS!"

More cheers. Tim decided to stay with the crowd, drink in the buzz.

"TkkDkkk Wkk BRkkNG Ykkk THk BkkG BLkkkk kkkX! MkkNTHS kkF WkRK kkND MkkLS kkF WkkkR HkkkV CkkM TkkkGkkTHkR kkND HkkR Wkkkk kkkkkR!"

He swept his hands toward the tent and out came the Big Blue Ox. Six wheels, one in front, one in back, the two on each side caterpillar-treaded. Blue paneling failed to fully hide the blackness of wires and tubes and hydraulics tucked behind. Atop the beast itself, a metal plate on carefully calibrated springs onto which was strapped three hundred pounds of equipment borrowed from the geology department plus batteries, since there's no sun indoors, duh.

"LkkT'S Gkkk THRkk THkkS TRkkkSH DkkSkRT kkND SkkkRCH FkR GkkLD!"

Phil held the remote over his head. The crowd hushed. He held it up to his face and squinted, then began a rapid manipulation of buttons and levers and the Big Blue Ox climbed over its first challenge, a trench of bent and twisted flatware. Any nerves Tim had over doing the public demonstration on an untested course dissipated. The Ox plowed straight through the Barbies making the crowd laugh, got a soiled dishtowel wrapped around a tread which it pulled off by extending the front wheel and spinning it off. That got applause, which made Tim smile since he was the one who had argued that feature was worth working into the design, even if it would never be used. Score!

The only moment of unease came when the Big Blue Ox nearly toppled down a sheer face of past-their-prime dinner plates, but the gyro came through just in time. This was the moment someone grabbed Tim's arm. He jumped, but his arm remained held. He turned to look. It was that dark-haired girl.

"You were right," she said. "This is cool."

"Thanks."

"Where'd you put the gyro?"

"What?"

"I'm just wondering if, with different placement, it might have corrected itself sooner."

Tim tipped his face and looked at her. Who was this girl? And why was she holding his arm?

"Maybe. Where would you put it?"

"I don't know. I haven't taken any classes or anything. Dead center?"

"What's your major?"

"MFHD."

"Huh." He turned back to watch the Big Blue Ox arrive back at the tent where Jesse made a show of patting and chucking it under the front wheel.

"Ykkk THkkkNK Wkk GkkkT kkk SHkkkkT?"

The crowd most certainly did.

$$\Delta x \Delta p \geq \frac{h}{4\pi}$$

Tim was waiting for that girl. Who was late. Which didn't surprise him. She seemed like the type. But he didn't want her to have to walk in alone. That's the worst. He heard some laughter muffled by the door and the opening of Weird Al's "Dare to Be Stupid"—a song to which it was impossible to dance frantically and maintain one's dignity. Which may be exactly why they started meetings that way. Tim didn't know. The song had been part of BYU's Fanciest Young Engineers Club longer than he had. FYEC FOEVAH!

Which. Hm. Maybe it was better that she was late. Would a foreigner understand a bunch of nerds jumping around and flailing their arms? And would a foreign *girl* make everyone too nervous to dance?

Fifteen minutes later he gave up and walked in and saw her sitting between Phil and that freshman kid whose name he could never remember. Abi or Ahab or Arab or—did that make him racist? Crap.

If his name didn't start with an A, this wouldn't be a problem. But maybe that's also racist? Crap.

She saw him and her face brightened—which hardly seemed possible given its base brightness—she jumped up and to him and took his arm. "See?" she said to everyone else. "The guy with a pocketknife!"

"We all have pocketknives," said Tim.

"Oh." She smiled and shrugged. "I tried."

"Well," said Phil, "we didn't have much business other than to pass a resolution in support of the Big Blue Ox team next weekend."

"That was very generous of us."

"I know, right?" Phil clapped his hands like a wind-up monkey. "So I guess we're ready for Oreos."

The girl frowned. "You mean—we don't get to dance again?"

Tim watched a look pass over each face in the room save his and hers. She must be some kind of dancer. He had better step in.

"No."

$$\vec{F} = m\,\vec{a}$$

She called Tim on Jesse's Blackberry the night after the competition as they relaxed in their Ridgecrest, CA 93555 hotel. She peppered him with questions till she knew the length of the trail (1.5km), changes in altitude (152m to 301m), the manner of scoring (confusing), who won (UCLA), how Purdue and Stanford did (3rd and 6th) and how the Big Blue Ox did (2nd) at which she squealed and congratulated him, and he reminded her that this was all costing Jesse money at which she apologized and recongratulated him and asked to apologize to Jesse.

"Here," said Tim.

"Hey," said Jesse.

Tim watched as Jesse tried to flirt over the crummy connection. "I *said* how *are* you" did not strike Tim as particularly winning, though what did he know? He sighed and trudged back inside to the remains of the buffet. A couple of gold-shirted Purdue guys were trying to peel tangerines dymaxionly. Tim stood next to them and started to pour himself a punch.

"Hey. BYU."

"Yeah?"

"Don't, man. One of the Florida kids spiked it. Vodka, I think."

"Oh. Thanks." Tim poured the punch back into the bowl and set the cup upside down next to it. Do they have any of those water bottles left?"

The Purdue guy pointed to the door. "They took them out into the lobby. Some people are playing *Ticket to Ride* and *Parthenon* out there."

"Thanks."

Sure enough, in the lobby where he'd just been walking three minutes ago were four players engaged in *Ticket to Ride* and a few others trying to figure out the rules to something Tim had never seen before. A dozen others were making MST3K-style commentary on the *T2R* players, and stacked next to them were all the unopened water bottles and candy bars. Tim walked over and grabbed a bottle and went to sit on the couch. A moment later he was joined on the far end by a girl in a bright yellow polo. "Cal Tech, right?" said Tim.

"Yes," she said. "And you're BYU though it says so on your shirt so it's no great deduction."

"You guys figure out what happened?"

"Yeah. Someone punctured a hole through the motherboard."

"Really?" Tim turned towards her. "Like, sabotage?"

"Probably. But we're pretty sure it happened before we came. Still. Who would do that?"

"Seriously." Tim shook his head and tipped back some

more water. "What kind of cutthroat culture you got over there at Cal Tech?"

She laughed. "Yeah, it's uh, it's—like the *Jaredites*. Right before they were destroyed. Not really of course. I'm just—you know—"

"You're Mormon."

"Yes!" She blushed. "Not that, you know, it matters or whatever."

"Are there a lot of Mormons at Cal Tech?"

"Yeah. I guess." She shrugged. "Not like BYU, of course."

"Of course."

They sat in silence. Tim sipped his water occasionally and looked at a painting of Joshua trees across the room. The Cal Tech girl fiddled with her watch. The game continued and the heckler's passions came and went in waves. Occasionally, a phone rang and the muffled voice of whoever was behind the desk replied.

"I'm Amy."

"Ampere Modulated Yielding."

"What?"

"Ampere's Law. It's, like, the magnetic equivalent of Gauss's Law."

"Oh."

She dug in her pockets, leaning back into the couch to get her hands in. Tim was vaguely aware of his brain cataloguing the way this pushed her breasts out. They were smallish, he supposed, but held high and prominent. Whether that was natural or a feat of brassiere engineering he had no way to know. Someday when he was married he would ask his wife about it. Maybe, you know, do some experiments or whatever.

"I'm going to get a Twix," he said. "Can I get you anything?"

She pulled out her hand and revealed five cat's-eye marbles in her fist. "Sure," she said. "Twix is good unless they have a Whatchamacallit. But no one ever does."

"Cool. When I get back, tell me about the marbles."

"Sure."

No Whatchamacallits and only one Twix left so he grabbed some Peanut M&M's. "They're out, so—" He opened up the Twix and gave her one. "I'm Tim."

"Maddie."

"I thought it was Amy."

"I always introduce myself first as Amy. I think it makes it easier for people to remember my real name—the dissonance, you know."

"Huh. You from California?"

"Berkeley. Total nerd ward. You?"

"Orem. Basketball ward."

"Sorry to hear that."

Tim shrugged and stuck half the Twix in his mouth. Which he chewed as he watched Maddie roll the five marbles around in her hand. He hadn't played marbles since— fifth grade?—but something about their equal and opposite reactions still captured his imagination. He ate the other half while she was still nibbling on the tip of hers, then broached the subject.

"So. Five marbles."

"Right." She looked around for the Twix wrapper, picked

it up and slid hers back in, then laid it on the arm of the couch. "Look. Pick one."

He did.

"Describe it."

"It's just a normal purple and orange cat's eye."

"Yep. Now, look at my hand. Notice anything?"

The four other marbles lay on her outstretched palm. The centers were different colors, but otherwise. . . . "No."

"Keep watching."

She rolled the marbles around in her hand. Tim watched. At first, nothing seemed unusual. But then he noticed that one marble moved less than the other three. In fact, it had hardly moved at all. He reached into her hand and pinched under the marble, against her skin, and lifted.

"Woah. It's heavy."

"Right. It's this superdense glass. I made it on my internship last summer at Corning. Cool, right?"

"Very. Have you played with it?"

"Yeah, but I didn't bring any shooters."

Tim smiled. She knew the difference. "'T's all right. Shall we try with those?"

She smiled back. "Okay."

They set up a circle with the peanut M&M's and put three of the marbles—including the heavy one—in the center.

Tim rocked back on his heels. "How about this? Displace an M&M with one of the center marbles, you get to eat it and go again. Displace any M&M with the one you're shooting, the other person eats it. Winner is the person to knock out the heavy marble.

"Sure. You want to go first?"

"No, no, no. Ladies first."

"They're my marbles. I decide. You go first."

Tim okayed as he rolled his marble between thumb and first two fingers. Then notched it in his index finger and shot it wildly to his left, sending three M&M's into Maddie's mouth.

"Thanks."

"It's been a long time."

She grinned. "Obviously." And shot out one of the lighter marbles. It gave her two more M&M's on its way. "Like that."

"You're some kind of shark, aren't you?"

She laughed and rocked backwards. "Your turn."

He was more careful this time, lining himself up, keeping his aim true. He hit a marble but his bounced right off.

"Ah. Right." And she knocked the last light marble out, flying over the M&M's.

"Can you knock it out?"

"It's not easy. Don't have much m so I need a lot of a. But more a means less accuracy, if you know what I mean." She cracked her marble against the heavy one, which barely rolled from the impact. The marble she shot bounced all the way back to her. She popped an M&M. "This'll take a while."

"So cool though. What do they use that glass for?"

"Industry secret. Which I think means they've invented it, just don't know what to use it for. They were telling me about this glass they invented years—decades?—ago that they're only now rolling out for a product. That too though is top secret. I have no idea what it'll be."

"Still cool though. I'm looking to get my first internship this summer. I hope something more closely related to, you know, *this*."

"Coming in second, that's got to be good, right?"

"Tim!"

Jesse burst into the lobby yelling, throwing out a few more Tim!s before finding them. "Hey," he said to Maddie, then: "You've got to tell me all about her."

"Who?"

"That girl who called you. On my phone? Like twenty minutes ago?"

"Oh. Her."

"Yes! Her!" To Maddie: "You have to understand. You have *never* seen a girl like this. I think I got pregnant just looking at her."

"Dude. She's Mormon."

Jesse blushed. "Sorry."

"And so are you."

"I guess we're even then. Start with her name. What's her name?"

"Don't know."

"'Don't know'? How the heck not? She's been with you *all* the *time* for a couple weeks. How the heck don't you know her name? Have you not looked at her? Gah! You're hopeless." And off he went.

"That was Jesse."

"He seems great."

Tim laughed. "Yeah. I guess."

"So . . ." Maddie wrinkled her nose. "Love triangle?"

Tim rolled his eyes. "Hardly. Jesse may love her but I know better. No way she loves either of us. She's just a tourist."

"What do you mean?"

Tim sighed and leaned against the couch. "She's—she's the sort of girl for whom high school-era categories are still useful. You know?"

"No. . . ."

"She's 'the popular girl'—a cheerleader type—she's the kind of girl people describe as effortlessly beautiful because no one can *try* to be that beautiful. I've never seen anyone like her and I wish she would just take off. I can't figure out what she wants, and she's making me nervous. Pretty sure she doesn't want Jesse though."

These were not thoughts Tim had thought before and he was surprised to hear them coming out of his mouth. But as he considered them, they seemed mostly true.

"Maybe she likes you."

Tim snorted. "Yeah. Right. I know it sounds negative, but I'm pretty sure she's taking advantage of me. I just can't figure out how."

"Geez. Paranoid much?" She threw a blue M&M at him which he caught against his chest and ate.

"Much."

"Well I just met you and I may never see you again, but you don't seem that hard to like to me."

Tim could feel his cheeks burn and he tried not to smile. Without looking up and in as offhand a manner as possible he said, "We should at least swap emails."

$$R_{\mu\nu} - \frac{1}{2}Rg_{\mu\nu} + \Lambda g_{\mu\nu} = \frac{8\pi G}{c^4}T_{\mu\nu}$$

But they forgot. They were up till 3am; BYU piled into the back of Brother Forester's old Ford van at 8am and it wasn't till 11am that Tim realized he'd never gotten her email. He imagined tracking her down and making some grand romantic gesture, but by the time they were back into Utah, her face had fully morphed into Amelia's and he was imagining this conversation:

"Hello. LDS Institute of . . . whatever city Cal Tech is in."

"Hi. I'm Tim Purdy. Don't know her last name but I'm looking for Amelia. I mean Maddie. Or was it Mandy? Anyway, it's not Amy, and she's an engineering student at Cal Tech."

Each time he imagined it, the conversation degraded more. It seemed to have a half-life of about a hundred miles.

So he dropped it.

Wasn't she just an Amelia substitute anyway? If he's going to be brave, shouldn't he be brave without the buffer of geography?

"Hey, Jesse?"

"Wuh?" Jesse turned from the front seat and looked back at Tim.

"Can I see your phone?"

"Um. Sure. Hang on." He spent a minute smacking the glove compartment until it opened. He took out a rockhard Red Vine and stuck it in his mouth, then grabbed his Blackberry and handed it back.

"Thanks."

He turned it on and found the list of incoming calls. Only three from yesterday, only one from the evening. He tried to call but the phone had no signal out here, so he just copied the number down.

$$\mu = GM$$

"Hello. You've reached Brick House. What do you want?"

"Hi. I'm Tim Purdy. I'm not sure the name of whom I'm calling."

"Then you must be looking for Julie."

"Oh? Why's that?"

"You saw her in what felt like a dream. A dream from which you will never awaken. Am I getting warm? And she never said her name?"

"What? No. Sheez. No. She's just always hanging around."

"That doesn't sound like Julie. What does she look like?"

"I don't know. She's . . . really pretty, I guess."

"Doesn't that describe us all."

"She had this pink and gray backpack. She carries around a socket wrench?"

"She carries that around with her? Huh. But yeah, that's Julie. She never reads her messages though so I'm not writing anything down for you."

Tim groaned and pulled at his hair. "Okay. Just—put it on her pillow. Just say 'Big Blue Ox Tim called.'"

"You sound desperate. Gotta warn you: she doesn't like that."

"Don't be weird. She's just always around so I thought I'd ask her advice on something."

"Whatever."

"Pillow."

"You got it, Romeo."

Tim's face collected around his nose. Females!

$$\sum \mathbf{F} = 0 \Rightarrow \frac{d\mathbf{v}}{dt} = 0$$

The stairs in the Clyde Building never felt as clean as BYU's reputation, but Tim still found himself sitting on them and eating his lunch as often as not.

"Hey."

He looked up and it was her. Julia? Crap. No time to check his notes. He chewed and swallowed. "Hey."

She sat down. Too close. He angled his knee away from her to keep their legs from touching all the way down.

Tim cleared his throat. "You, ah, got my message?"

"Yes." She pulled it from her breast pocket and read it to him, then touched his elbow and leaned closer. He was right against the banister and couldn't get away. "Thank you. You're a hard catch."

Tim's eyebrows revealed his skepticism, but he went on. "I need to ask you something."

"Sure. Just ask for something small. Nothing turns a girl off faster than a proposal at the end of date one. No matter how interested she was before."

"What? No!" Tim bonked his head against the handrail. "What are you talking about?"

She folded her hands in her lap. "Nothing. Just listening."

"Okay. So there's this girl."

"Of course." She winked at him and he lost his way.

"Ummmm."

"This girl?"

"Right. So there's this girl. And she's . . . awesome? And I think—I think probably you know like every guy in the department's had a crush on her—"

"I'm sorry."

"Not your fault, I just—" breath "—she—" breath "—I—she's simply amazing. She's pretty and smart—"

"How did you—?"

"—and frankly I don't even—" breath "—how'm I supposed to approach her?"

The girl frowned. "I'm confused."

Tim snorted a laugh at himself. "I did it again, didn't I?"

"What do you mean?"

Tim ran a hand through his hair. "This thing where I'm almost hyperventilating. It happens every time I talk about her. Which is why I don't. Not often. Gah! How'm I even supposed to be able to talk *to* her?"

The girl looked at him a long time, her brow furrowed. If he'd been looking in a mirror, Tim would've assumed he was doing linear algebra. Finally she nodded and scooted a bit away from him so she could face him more directly, look into his eyes. She grabbed his hands and held them over his knees. Softly, "You can talk to her. You talk to me just fine."

At this Tim laughed a brief but more genuine laugh and pulled his hands back. "That's totally different. I don't have to impress *you*."

"You don't?" She turned to watch a kid struggling not to drop his stack of seven textbooks. "Why not?"

"Why would I? There's no chance of us ever ending up together. You're not looking for an engineer. Be serious."

She frowned and looked at the stair between her feet. "I like engineering."

"It's not the same thing. You'll graduate and get a subscription to *Wired* or something and be satisfied. You'll get bored of hanging with us soon enough."

"You think?"

"I know." Tim patted her shoulder. "You go after what interests you and it's okay because everyone's interested *in* you. The world, as they say, is your oyster."

"What do you know? I can't have you."

"Meh. Hypotheticals." He was about to roll his eyes when he noticed her stillness. "Are you—okay?"

In one fluid moment she took his chin and kissed him softly. Her eyes held his and their . . . *knowingness* calmed him at about the halfway point. When she pulled away, a soft sound accompanied their lips' separation. She raised an eyebrow. "How was that?"

"I, uh, you, why, you, I, how, uh."

"You still want to get her?"

"Y-yes?"

She nodded. "Then be bold. Don't do what I just did, but take a chance. You can do that?"

"I—guess?"

"You can. Go."

Tim stood and stumbled away, his bag in one hand, not fully zipped. Four or five paces away he turned back and looked at her. She sat next to his sandwich, eyes in her lap. Then she reached down and unzipped her bag's front pocket and removed her socket wrench and tossed it in the air. It made three lazy loops before landing in her hand. She spun it through her fingers and dropped it back in her bag.

Tim turned away. It seemed too personal to watch.

$$\frac{\partial u}{\partial t} - \alpha \left(\frac{\partial^2 u}{\partial x^2} + \frac{\partial^2 u}{\partial y^2} + \frac{\partial^2 u}{\partial z^2} \right) = 0$$

Amelia was sitting in an empty classroom with a couple other members of the Nut Caucus. Her hair was unbound and veiling her face which was bent over the paper she was working something out on. The other two girls were sitting on desks and looking at him.

"Um. Amelia?"

She looked up and the fluorescent tubes reflected in her eyes. She was wearing a light green tshirt with a TARDIS on it. Her peacoat was on the chair beside her. She rested an arm on it and gestured with her other. "Yes?"

"Could I talk to you just a minute?"

She looked at her two friends. They shrugged at her so she pushed her chair away and stood up. On her walk to the door, the backend of Tim's mind started calculating her every feature. He pinched his eyes shut for a moment to push back the panic. He thought of the kiss. He opened his eyes and watched Amelia stop in front of him, fold her arms and put all her weight on her right leg, cocking out her left hip. "What's up, Tim?"

"I'm Tim."

"I know. Unlike you, I know people's names."

"I remember your name."

"Sorry. I'm not trying to be rude. This heat distribution's just giving me some trouble. What's up?"

Tim touched his chin, letting a knuckle touch his lips. "Right. So, Saturday I'm going into Salt Lake for a lecture on freeway design at the U. You want to come?"

"Who else is going?"

"Nobody."

Amelia tilted her head and looked at him more closely. She moved her hands to her back pockets.

"If you don't want to—"

"No. No, that sounds cool. What time you want to pick me up?"

"Six? Where will you be?"

"Give me a call. Here:" She took his hand and pulled a ballpoint pen from her pocket and wrote 3772415 on his wrist.

"Cool. Should I call tonight so we can make arrangements? Then I'll see you Saturday?"

"Sounds good. I'll be home by nine, nine thirty."

Tim sort of saluted and stepped backwards out the door. When he heard it shut he pumped the air with his fists.

"Success?"

That girl—Julia?—was standing about fifteen feet away.

"Yeah. Thanks. Did—did you know that would work?"

She shrugged. "We all have our talents."

"Well, she said yes. We're going to Salt Lake on Saturday."

"Congratulations."

"I owe you one."

She laughed and rolled her head back. She did have a beautiful laugh. "I just may hold you to that."

"I hope so. Though what could I do for you?"

"What indeed."

They regarded each other a moment, then Tim nodded, said see you later, and walked away from her, down the hallway, around the corner, away.

Meet The Nut Caucus

In engineering you fail
all of the time.
—Bryan Catanzaro

AMELIA

"Hi?"

Amelia and Ruth and Bets jerked their heads toward the door. This time it was a girl, but none of them recognized her.

"Hello?" offered Ruth.

"Can I come in?"

"Sure." Ruth stood up and waved her in. "Come on. Are you interested in the Nut Caucus?"

"The what?"

Amelia regarded the girl. She was dressed practically but still looked expensive in a can-you-support-my-daughter-in-the-manner-she-has-become-accustomed sort of way. "It's the club for female engineers. We're usually here Thursday afternoons."

"Is this all of you?"

"Who bother to come," said Bets with an exaggerated eyeroll.

"Huh." The girl walked the rest of the way in and sat at a desk near them. "I'm Julie."

Bets pursed her face. "You got a last name, Julie?"

"Yes. But it's hard to pronounce."

"Heaven forbid we learn something hard."

Ruth cut in. "Don't mind Bets. I'm Ruth. And this is Amelia."

"Hi."

"Hi." Amelia nodded at her. "So . . . if you didn't know we were here, are you just opening random doors?"

"No, I—This will sound weird, but I was following Tim."

Bets turned back, her face wide. "Tim? Who was just here? You were following *that* Tim? Tim probably-doesn't-know-your-name Tim?"

Julie blushed slightly. "I know."

"Well," said Bets. "He was after Amelia, if you must know. Has been for a while, though we weren't sure he would ever make a move."

"So—" Julie seemed to consider this "—it was welcome?"

Amelia's face scrunched up. "Not exactly. But I'm glad he finally made a move. Now something can happen or not happen and we can be done with it."

"Or not," added Julie.

Amelia nodded and shrugged in a single thought.

Julie's fingers twitched over the front pocket of her backpack. She craned her neck to look at the graph paper Amelia'd been writing on. "So what do you do?"

Amelia shrugged. "Mostly thought experiments."

"For instance."

"Today we're considering options for keeping yurts cool on Venus. Super-useful stuff."

"Awesome. It's like . . . a dream. You just sit here. Doing math."

Ruth nodded in a sharp certain motion. "We have to. We're surrounded by males all day long. Our proportion is way lower than at other schools. And it's low at other schools!"

Julie nodded, matching Ruth's manner. "I didn't even think of signing up for engineering. Somehow it just—I don't know—didn't seem like the place for me."

Bets looked up from the pencil whose eraser she was picking apart. "Maybe it's not."

"C'mon, Bets," said Ruth. "Knock it off." She turned to Julie. "Even if you're not in the major you can still come to the Nut Caucus."

Julie opened and closed the zipper of her bag. "What does that name mean?"

Bets pulled a paper from the binder on the desk next to her. It was an 8.5×11 piece of copypaper. "Th7-8" and "Clyde 245" were written along the bottom, and a nut, sitting on top of a Red Cross-like cross, took up the bulk of the page. It looked like clipart, a hexagonal nut in stark black and white, threads just visible in the center.

"It—?" said Julie, pointing. Then she got it. "It's the female symbol with a nut."

"Nice job, Nancy Drew," said Bets. "But of all the hardware in the world, why a nut?"

"It's just, uh, a basic . . . building block . . . symbol of . . . engineering. . . ."

"Bets," said Ruth. "Knock it off."

Amelia sighed and cut in. "What Bets is trying to embarrass you with is that it's essentially a sex joke. Nuts are female, ha oh ha, just like bolts are male."

Julie nodded. "I get it. Why would I be embarrassed?"

Amelia shrugged. "Search me. But Bets is convinced our charter will be revoked if BYUSA ever catches on."

Bets rerolled her eyes. "'Convinced' is a strong word."

"Nut Caucus. I like it. Exceedingly subtle." Julie grinned. "I had no idea BYU's lady engineers could be so wicked."

"Actually," said Bets, "the preferred term is bitch engineers."

"Actually," said Amelia, "the preferred term is engineers."

"I like," said Julie. "And I concur. For what it's worth."

All four of them leaned back and looked at each other. The silence lengthened until Bets started making faces. Finally she hit on one that set Ruth alaughing. Amelia and Julie joined in. The laughter burnt out quickly and Amelia turned to Julie. "So tell us—what brings you to the Nut Caucus. And don't say Tim. I'm speaking more . . . cosmologically."

Julie tilted her face. "You mean . . . makeup?"

Amelia turned to her friends. "Is that what I said?"

Bets shrugged. Ruth said, "I still don't know why cosmic understanding and mascara are almost the same word."

Julie laughed and hid her face behind a hand. "Ah, geez. Right. Sorry." She looked up. "I just confirmed everything you think about me, huh?"

Amelia smiled and reached out to push Julie's shoulder. "It's all right."

"I don't know if I have a good reason."

"Then it is, truly, cosmic." Amelia stood and walked to the front of the room, found a piece of chalk and wrote COSMIC NUT CAUCUS in big letters on the board. "What do you think?"

Bets rolled her eyes again, disappearing them into her black bangs. "Now you're just being gross."

"I like it," said Ruth. She giggled. "The glory of God is intelligence, right? And who's smart? We're smart!"

The Nut Caucus laughed and Julie smiled. "You meet here every Thursday?"

Ruth nodded. "Every Thursday."

"And Bets won't be upset if I return?" Julie winked at Bets, who frowned in reply.

"Whatever."

"Great. Do you know what we'll be talking about next week? So I can read up?"

"Um . . ." Amelia looked at the others who shrugged. "Why don't you bring something you're interested in? We'll see if we can't help."

"Really?" Julie clapped her hands in an upsettingly girlish manner. "Cool! Thanks!"

And off she went.

Amelia walked her to the door, then walked back to Bets and Ruth at a distracted saunter. "Huh."

Bets grunted. "Huh indeed."

Ruth itched the bridge of her nose, then came up with, "What a brave new world that has such people in it."

RUTH

Ruth had a theory about why skirts are appropriate for church and pants are not. Actually, she had three theories, each sillier than the last. Skirts are more appropriate than pants because it's easier to lap-catch angels toppling from heaven when wearing a skirt. Skirts are more appropriate than pants because the extra fabric can be used to clothe the poor and fatherless should you happen upon some. Skirts are more appropriate than pants because it's easier to remember your nakedness before God when your naked legs are rubbing against each other.

She giggled then turned back to the bathroom mirror to watch herself as she put on mascara. Ruth also had a theory about makeup, viz. never use more than two types of makeup at once. Not including foundation, but Ruth had a theory that foundation should not be used before age thirty unless you're . . . unfortunate. Which makeups are the best two makeups—so to speak—was the real question under investigation. Today she was back to mascara and blush. She had a new, orangier blush she was interested in trying out. Her investigation would get along much quicker if she wore makeup every day, but who has time for that?

Besides, her test population was a mess. Her ward had been seeing her for weeks and weeks now and since everyone knew her, what different effect could she really hope for? What she really needed was to visit a different ward every week and see how many boys approached her. Or girls shunned her. That might be fun. Ruth practiced her wicked grin and screwed shut the mascara. She tore the plastic from the blush and popped it open to blinding orangity. She had a feeling she'd just flushed three bucks. But no turning back now.

Besides. While she couldn't skip her own ward every week and hope to keep her ecclesiastical endorsement, today she had a legitimate excuse. An old friend from freshman year was going on a mission at the end of the semester and was speaking today. Not a stellar excuse, really, but a legitimate one.

She arrived six minutes early and checked her counting mechanism before going in. It was a simple device. She just bumped her wrist against her waist and it registered one more. Sort of like an odometer. Without being anything like an odometer. Her goal was to have at least five boys approach her. That was base level. With luck, no one here knew her. That would throw off the data. And someday when her research was completed she could write a paper discussing which makeup combinations were most attractive, and whether to cads or, you know, decent human beings. Ruth had a secret theory she even kept mostly from herself: all boys are cads. It was not one she believed, but she wasn't sure what the purpose of makeup was otherwise. But if she'd wanted to know *that* she would have gone into evolutionary biology or behavioral psychology or something. Really, this whole thing was just an excuse to make concealed gadgets to input information onto. Exactly the same reason she was studying the number of words in the opening and closing prayers at Devotional or how visibly hand-holding was being conducted at ward prayer. Essentially, she just liked to record information people wouldn't like to know she was recording. Consider the box of sorted-by-color pens she'd been "borrowing" since high school. But do not consider the sorted-by-color used tissues her mother found in her backpack in third grade. Even 2005 Ruth thinks that's gross. At least, she thinks, 1993 Ruth could have invested in a nice box of latex gloves first.

The first gentleman to approach her may have been assigned usher duties, but Ruth counted him anyway, enjoying the pleasant clunk of tumblers as her counter moved from 0000 to 0001. She explained what she was doing there (the excuse, not the reason), and he welcomed her and, for one moment, his eyes were everywhere but her face. Yes. This certainly counted. She walked into the auditorium that served as chapel. The place was filling up, but she walked past the handful of folding chairs and chose a plush seat without further accostment. Such a deliberate and nonrandom choice reminded her of the real problem with her methodology: she was hardly doing this double-blind. Ruth, she said to herself, you are a terrible scientist. Which made her so happy.

"You look happy."

"I *am*, thank you!"

0002

"I don't think we've met. I'm Charlie." He leaned over the chair next to her and shook her hand.

"Ruth. But we haven't met because this isn't my ward. I'm just here for Danielle Kunz. Do you know her?"

"I know the name." He looked skyward as if trying to remember more than that and Ruth took the opportunity to look him over. When he looked back down, her eyes were ready to meet his. "Dark hair, I think? Education major of some sort?"

"That's the one." Ruth smiled and Charlie hopped the row to sit next to her.

"This seat's not taken?"

"I only need one."

"Great."

Ruth glanced forward and saw the meeting was ready to start. The bishop or whoever was at the pulpit and the final measure of "How Great Thou Art" was plodding to a close. Aaand they were off. Only two before church, but she had three hours to go, one of which might be entirely flirt-filled. So not a bad start.

After the sacrament, Danielle spoke first. She gave a dull sermon that lost Ruth somewhere between Galilee and Ghana, and Ruth started to examine the rest of the ward. After a moment, she noticed Charlie's attention locked in a single direction. She followed his gaze to a head of hair half-put-up, half falling across a green-clad back. Even with those few details, she recognized Julie immediately. She slid her eyes back to Charlie then across the congregation. He was the only one outright staring, but several eyes kept sliding Julie's direction.

Ruth slipped out her notebook and wrote "ask J makeup q."

Danielle was crying now and in a game attempt at solidarity, Ruth looked at her as she blurbled through something about her mother and her roommates and Jesus. Pretty inspiring stuff. And massive mascara rivers to boot.

"ask D makeup q"

A hundred forty minutes and a slip out a side door later, Ruth pulled back her sleeve to see 0014. Very good. But not as good as a certain someone else. Maybe, before next Sunday, she would make a counter less topheavy with zeroes.

BETS

Bets, as a matter of lone-wolf principle, refused to participate in FHE activities. The whole concept of her ecclesiastical unit sticking her in a phony family was distasteful, artificial. That she happened to like pretty much everyone in her FHE group made this principled stance less enjoyable. That Rootbeeragogo had an every-week 20-people-for-the-price-of-five Family-Home-Evening Monday-Night Special with great bands was a related problem. But if she happened to show up and the rest of them just happened to be there, well, score one for God. Bets didn't begrudge him the occasional victory.

Bets loved going to shows not just because, you know, *music*, but also because Rootbeeragogo was about the only place she felt free to put on her full Bettie Page regalia and, thus, instead of seeing "there goes fat girl" in people's eyes, seeing "holy smokes: Bettie Page." She took as fact that all men of her generation took a moment now and then to look at naked women on the Internet, and, thankfully, Bettie Page was now online, doing her duty for nonanorexics everywhere, may she live forever.

Anyway, nylons with a line down the back, black dress with white polka dots, lipstick red enough to cause cancer.

Show up first, sit at the bar, sip a mocktail by the straw, cross your legs, wag your foot. It's like performance art, her roommate once said. Bets wouldn't know about that. She was an engineer, dammit.

She sipped her hilariously named Abstinence on the Beach by the straw and watched for people she knew as she listened to OK Ikumi set up their synthesizers. Not her favorite instrument, but she liked the other two bands on the docket immensely. My Bloody Fingers was new but awesome and Sunfall Festival was one bit of luck away from fame and fortune. Bets tried not to begrudge them that too much. At least she could say she knew them when. In the meantime she would look for Mary from My Bloody Fingers or Amy from Sunfall Festival and say hi or whatever. Know one person from each local band you like. Advice from an uncle. Probably the best advice anyone gave her before starting college.

A couple of guys—coincidentally from her FHE group! what were the odds!—came in and sat next to her and started chatting her up. They were both idiots, but the kind of idiot that's easy to like and fun to talk to. They had crazy (read: stupid) ideas about computers and traffic lights and hairspray flamethrowers, but she had a hard time hating them. In fact, she'd given up trying. Pure innocence was too rare in this world and should be treasured.

While one of them was talking about the new *Dukes of Hazzard* movie, she let her gaze wander from his empty blue eyes and across the room. The bassist of My Bloody Fingers was walking in with a girl wearing a cheap, plastic, kitten mask. Bets recognized her immediately. It was that girl who crashed Nut Caucus. She moved as lithely as her mask suggested she might, while the bassist kept bumping her case into chairs. The girl skipped ahead and started clearing a path. Bets could hear them laughing but not what they were saying.

"Yeah, but, dude—it can't be better than *Starsky & Hutch*. That movie had Snoop in it."

Bets looked back at them. "Snoop?" she said.

"Yeah. He's a rapper."

The other one shook his head sadly. "He's a pothead too, dude."

"Yeah, but. There's like a huge correlization between those things. There are no coincidences in life, dude."

"That's what you said about finding that Joseph Smith pamphlet when you were in high school."

"Yeah, man. So?"

"So why would God get you the Church and get Snoop pot? That dun't make sense."

Bets held up a hand, and they turned to her expectantly. "I think I got this one. God can only give us what we're ready for. You, being a kid of great wisdom and maturity, were given the gospel. Snoop Dog, being less prepared, was given pot. A stepping stone until he is ready for further enlightenment."

"Whoa," said one.

"Dude," said the other.

Bets gave herself ten points.

"But if you'll excuse me," she said, "I need to say hello to someone."

She stood and walked away, making sure to sashay enough swish into her skirt to swing it as widely as possible. Her captain dress—centerpiece of her #3 Bettie Page look—couldn't do this. But it was much tighter. To each according to its strengths. Just like Snoop and his smokes.

The kitten saw her coming first. "Bets!" she said, holding her arms out in an ambiguous gesture that might or might not have been an invitation to hug. Bets decided to force the latter interpretation and threw her hands up also and said, "Hi!"

"Oh, the mask, right. It's Julie."

"I know. I recognized you."

"You look great!"

"Thanks."

Julie pulled the bass player forward a step. "Have you come to hear My Bloody Fingers? This is Heather. She's their bass player."

Heather nodded at Bets. "Hence the bass case."

"Heather, this is Bets. She's an engineer."

"Oh, cool. Do you— I mean, we're not about to record an album or anything, but do you think—"

Bets held up a hand. "I'm not that kind of engineer. I'm more into building things with cement."

"Oh. 'Kay." She shifted the case. "I gotta go see if Mary or Jessica's backstage. I'll be back though to watch OK Ikumi, okay?"

"Cool. See you then." Julie watched her walk backstage, then turned to Bets. "What you drinking?"

Bets looked at what was in her hand. "I—can't remember," she lied.

"I think it might be an Abstinence on the Beach?"

"You're the expert."

"I've wondered if the real cocktail is Sex at the Beach or Absinthe on the Beach. What do you think?"

Bets cocked her head and looked at Julie. Even with the kitten face (especially with the kitten face?) there was something . . . *too much* about her. "I haven't really thought about it. Do you come here much?"

"Mm." Julie shrugged. "Now and then. This is my . . . third time?"

"But you know all the drinks?"

"Ugh. It's not like *I'm* buying them, believe me. Never have more than two or all you'll want to do is rub your tongue with sandpaper. They're deadly sweet." She stuck her tongue out which weirdly heightened the cat effect. Bets looked over her shoulder and saw that—what a coincidence!—a couple of her FHE sisters had taken up with the dopes she'd left at the bar. She jerked her thumb at them.

"Sorry, I gotta jet. FHE."

Julie nodded. "Yeah, my group did frisbee golf earlier. Somehow I didn't feel like it."

"Okay. Well. Bye." Bets walked backwards a few steps until Julie waved, then she turned and walked to the bar. The conversation had moved to ward gossip—were Brad and Suzy engaged?—would Shaunee keep waiting for her missionary now that Robert was plying her with charm? Important stuff like that. Bets set her drink down and pushed it away.

Blue eyes asked her if she was going to finish it. She waved her wrist. "Please. But unless you want to be accused of kissing me, don't use the straw. That's a potent lipstick mark."

He laughed. "That would be awesome! I mean, uh. Do you want to kiss? Because, uh, you know, if—" He looked around at everyone else and blushed. It was adorable. "I'll be careful," he said and downed it in one go. "What's this one called?"

"Abstinence on the Beach."

Everyone laughed at him as he blushed again. Bets leaned back against the bar. "It's not a curse," she said. "Or, if it is, I release you from said curse."

"Cool. Thanks."

She shook her head. He had no bleeding idea what was going on.

AMELIA

Although she hardly thought about the Nut Caucus most of the week, as soon as she walked in, Amelia felt a weight lift off her shoulders. "I'm here," she said to no one but herself.

Which was good because Bets and Ruth were in the middle of a surprisingly loud conversation. "She did not!" said Ruth.

"She did," said Bets.

"Who did what?" asked Amelia, walking closer.

"I don't know!" said Ruth. "But Julie!"

"What?"

Bets explained: "I was just telling Ruth that I saw that Julie person on Monday at a music thing and she was wearing a cat mask."

"A cat mask?"

"Masquerade style. Plastic. With whiskers."

Amelia's face was a blank.

"I know, right?" said Ruth. "And at church she wa—"

"She's in your ward?"

"No, no, no." Ruth patted Amelia's arm. "I was visiting another ward. But that's not the point."

"What did she do?"

Ruth scrunched her nose in thought. "It wasn't so much that she *did* anything. It was more like—"

The door opened and all three looked over to see Julie walking in. "Hey, guys," she said. "I don't think I'm late?"

"She came," said Bets.

Amelia elbowed her. "No, you're fine. I just got here. You bring anything to work on?"

"I think so. Hopefully it's not too boring for you." She shut the door behind her without so much as a click and walked over, swinging her backpack off as she came. "How was your date?"

"What?"

"That's right!" said Ruth. "How did I forget to ask you in class? Tim!"

"Oh, right." Amelia nodded. "Actually, pretty good. I sort of hope he maybe asks me out again."

Bets snorted. "Right. Like there's any chance of him *not* doing that."

Amelia. "I don't know. He's surprisingly hard to read one-on-one."

"Sounds hot." Bets grinned at her.

"Oh, shut up."

Julie dropped into a chair by Amelia. "Cool. Good luck."

Ruth cleared her throat. "Happy that we're not too happy, lucky that we're not too lucky."

Amelia looked at her. "I don't know that one."

"It's from *Hamlet*. Which is pretty much the luckiest bit of literature I can think of."

They all nodded somberly, then looked at each other and snickered.

"Anyway," said Amelia. "I don't have much else to say at this point. Except wait and see."

"If that's an engineering joke," said Bets, "I'm offended."

Amelia laughed. "Fair enough. What you got, Jules?"

"Okay. I don't know. Maybe I should be embarrassed about this?" She opened her backpack and pulled out an ancient book. "1920," she said in reply to their faces. "*Text Book of Applied Aeronautic Engineering*."

Ruth reached out and touched it. "Where did you *find* this?"

"DI. Thrift store of the gods. It's where I get all my engineering and math stuff from. Since I'm not taking classes, I don't have to buy the hundred-fifty-buck books."

"You're missing out," grunted Bets.

"Anyway, planes weren't all that complicated in 1920. But check out this picture of the 'Tarrant "Tabor" Triplane.' Cool, right?"

The Nut Caucus oohed and ahed appreciatively.

"Anyway, I was trying to figure out the drag force with the three wings and six engines and stuff and then plug that into what I know about aerodynamics generally. I think I have it right enough, but my physics is of the sort where I'm best at figuring out how perfect spheres behave in a vacuum. This thing's got way more pieces than I really know how to describe mathematically. Let alone fit in actual air and whatever."

"Let's see your math," said Amelia.

Julie pulled out a notebook, turned it to the right page, and started to hand it to Amelia, but Bets snatched it away. "Let me see it. Amelia already knows this stuff. I'm in an aeronautics class now." She looked it over. "I have no idea what the hell you're doing here."

"Yeah." Julie frowned. "I was afraid of that. I think most of what I know isn't actually very practical. It's physics, not engineering. If you know what I mean."

"Yeah," said Amelia. She took the notebook from Bets and started running a finger across the page. "Wow. This is pretty good, Jules. Ruth. Check this out."

Ruth leaned over and Amelia tilted the paper at her. "What am I looking at?"

"You name it." Ruth and Amelia examined the paper in silence for a few minutes. Amelia finally looked up. "You did this with what you got in high school?"

"Basically, I guess."

"Your high school was better than mine."

"I mean—I do buy these things. Most of them are more regular textbooks, but they're all from, like, the '70s. I don't know how up-to-date they are."

Amelia hummed and went back to the notebook. "Doesn't matter, really. Principles don't change. New materials, new codes. That stuff changes. Reality doesn't change. You seem to have a pretty good grasp on reality."

"You mind telling me what she did there?"

"Sorry, Bets." Amelia scooted over to her and started pointing out things on the page. Ruth leaned towards Julie.

"You're pretty good. I mean—sure, there're some numbskull errors in there, but you've got the basics down. I couldn't have done so well freshman year and I declared before I even showed up in the dorms. Nice work."

"Thanks."

Amelia listened to Ruth complimenting Julie as she pulled out a pen and started correcting her figures. After a couple corrections, Bets was able to do most of the rest herself. Then she leaned back and asked Julie if she wanted a formula for shortcutting air issues. "This isn't exact. The FAA won't let you sell to Delta, but it'll get you through a first product-pitch with your boss."

"Cool."

Before Amelia realized it, ninety minutes had passed and Bets and Ruth were gone. "Crap. Sorry. I love teaching people stuff."

"No, this was great. I haven't actually been taught something this meaty in a while."

"Cool. Because you're never getting these couple hours back. But I got to go. You coming next week?"

"You bet."

"Bring something again."

"Okay."

Julie packed up and left. Amelia sat and stretched. She had to be careful. The last thing she wanted was to end up teaching. The world needs more women engineers. Not more women teachers. Don't take steps toward someone else's future.

Her phone buzzed. It was Tim. She silenced it and continued staring at the wall.

Meet A Bechdel Proctor

Anastasia pushed open the front door. The room was empty except for Julie, sitting on the couch, lost yet again in some dense, published-in-the-'70s textbook from a field she wasn't even studying.

"Where are the twins?"

Julie jerked up, wide-eyed.

"Did I startle you?"

She nodded.

"Sorry. Where're the twins?"

"Don't know."

"Good. You're coming with me to Costco."

"Am I?"

"You are. They're not invited because they're hopeless. You, though. You just keep getting more interesting. And experience shows that the best way to get a relationship to finally pass the Bechdel test is to take the woman to Costco."

"The what?"

"I'll explain. Right now all you need to know is I have a membership and you don't and it's Saturday so there'll be lots of samples. Let's go."

Julie bent a page in her book and set it on the couch. Anastasia noticed the placement because usually Julie hid them in case any boys happened by. She then stood and walked to the door and put on her shoes.

"Should I grab my purse?"

"Up to you. I'm not going to make you buy anything."

Julie nodded then ran to her room, returning with her debit card held in the air.

They walked out and nearly bumped into the two football players who'd been coming around lately and their scrawny roommate Randy.

"Oh, uh, hey," said Anderson. "You, uh, headed out?"

"Yes," said Anastasia. "Bad luck, boys. May it be better next time."

"We, uh, come with you?"

"No, sorry, members only."

Julie blessed them with a sad look and followed Anastasia down the stairs and into her paint-peeling '92 Corolla.

"Lock your door."

She did, put on her seatbelt, and waved at the boys. Who were, Anastasia was certain, looking at the shadows now made by the strap bisecting Julie's bosom.

"Let's go." Anastasia forced the car into reverse. She waited for the clunk, then craned her neck and backed onto 200 East. She then clunked it into drive and off they went to the Orem Costco.

"I never see you go to Costco," said Julie as they turned onto University.

"How do you mean."

"I never see you leave and I never see you come back. Just every once in a while there are big empty boxes in the trash."

"I'm very silent."

"Like a vampire."

Anastasia barked a single laugh. "Or something."

"How's your thesis coming?"

Anastasia watched University Avenue become University Parkway become part of Orem. "It's coming." This answer was unsatisfying so she tried again: "It's coming."

They pulled into the Costco lot and Anastasia grabbed a cart as she flashed her card and they walked inside. "I'm mostly just here for quote feminine unquote products, but I think I might get a pie and scope out the media while I'm here. I'm all caught up on Lauren Hamilton and Anne Rice but you never know. Might be something cool. They haven't had any good DVDs for a while."

"Sounds good." Julie ran her fingers along kids shoes and face lotions. "Maybe I'll get something chocolate."

"Always a good plan."

They passed by the photo desk and rows of tvs. Julie paused at a laptop and rubbed her finger back and forth across the trackpad. Anastasia watched her.

"It's a pretty great price," said Julie.

"Yes."

"If you have a job."

Anastasia laughed. "Or you could take up a collection. You could have it by tomorrow."

Julie dropped her hands to her side. "Yeah." She clenched her fists. "I'm so sick of. . . . It's not like it means anything."

Anastasia had emphatically *not* come here to talk about boys but this was exactly what she wanted to know. "But . . . you're here to get married."

"Isn't everybody? But it's also a university, right? And a good one. You're supposed to work for things. What am I working for?"

"Before you, Julie, I thought MFHD was a throwaway major. But you're always working on something. When you're not reading old math books. Or going on three dates a night."

"I haven't done that in a couple months."

"Only because you've started saying no. You never used to say no."

"Yeah. . . ." Julie sped past the rest of the computers and the cellphone kiosk where the face of the guy standing there convulsed at the sight of her. But who needs a phone when everyone comes to you?

Anastasia skipped a step to catch up with her. The burst of speed revealed a bad wheel, and the cart tried to ram the cellphone guy. She yanked it back in line and caught up to Julie. "Hey, hey, hey. That's not why we came here. We came to shop in bulk and screw boys. No, wait—"

Julie laughed and took her arm. "Exactly! That's exactly it! Now. Tell me about this test. It's like a logic puzzle?"

"Test—? Oh, right. Sort of, I guess." Anastasia took a sudden left past a huge stack of women's sweaters and pointed at a similarly sized stack of women's trenchcoats. "What do you think?"

"They're nice. Khaki or black or navy?"

"Black, definitely. Black black black. And I can afford it, but it'll blow my budget for this month and next. What do you think?"

"Try it on."

Anastasia lifted her purse off her shoulder and dropped it in the cart. She hunted through the stack for her size. Only one: the last black before she hit the table; she'd have to decide today. She yanked it out, trying to send as few other coats to the floor as possible. She put it on. Turned around. Hands in pockets, hands out of pockets. Buttons. Belt. Collar up, collar down. "What do you think?"

"I think this is what you're supposed to look like."

"Is it worth the money?"

"I can't answer that." Julie made a circuit, examining Anastasia slowly from collar to hem. "Leave it on while we shop."

"Why?"

"If you get more comfortable, it's yours. If you can't stop thinking about the money, leave it here."

Anastasia nodded. "Okay." She flipped the cart around and pushed it back into the main aisle. They paused next at a glass case filled with ice and lobster tails. Anastasia snorted. "Cockroach of the sea."

"But delicious."

"Still." Anastasia scratched her neck where the plastic thingey was holding the pricetag. "So the Bechdel test was invented by Alison Bechdel who does this comic about lesbians."

"So this is a test about being lesbian? Because I've seen you making out with that Dutch grad student. Pretty sure you're straight. Potato-salad sample?"

"Ew. No. People thinking you might be a lesbian does not make it any less fun to make people think you might be a lesbian."

"Whatever, Anastasia. Does that even make sense? So. Lesbian test. Should I be scandalized?"

"Not hardly. Actually, it's pretty boring. The point is, in one strip—"

"Ha, ha. Strip."

"Ha ha." Anastasia slugged her. "Knock it off. In one strip there's this test for judging movies."

"Okay."

"Does the movie have two named female characters who talk to each other about something other than a man."

Julie frowned. "That's it? That's a pretty low bar."

"You would think so. What's your favorite movie?"

"I'm still on the high *Ocean's Eleven* started in high school."

"Fails."

"Okay, um. *About a Boy*? I guess maybe not. *Legally Blonde*? Surely—? I need to watch it again. I'm not sure. But surely—"

"Higher bar than you thought."

"I got it." She slapped the cart's handlebar. "*A League of Their Own*."

"That sounds likely. I've never seen it, though."

"Yeah. Me neither."

Anastasia laughed and pushed the cart toward the fancy cheeses. "Coat or no coat, I haven't bought brie this entire semester. I'm getting some brie."

"Look at us!" said Julie, jumping and clapping. "We're talking about fancy fresh cheeses! And cheeses aren't men!"

"Seriously. If I ever have a daughter, I'm naming her Brie."

"Assuming she's cute enough to eat right up?"

"Yes." Anastasia paused just long enough to grab a wedge. "Assuming that."

Julie swept the brie from the cart and started reading the wrapper. "In high school, just after my brother Tom came home from his mission, he took me to LA, and I bought some brie because my friends were always talking about it, but I'd never had any. I left it in the hotel while we went to Knott's Berry Farm. Anyway, I twisted my ankle at the twisted-perspective house and we went back early. Stupidly, I'd left the cheese on the windowsill, but while I was icing my ankle I reached over and grabbed it and opened it. I didn't know about soft cheeses so I tried to break off a chunk but it was melted inside and splooshed all over my shirt."

"What did your brother say?"

"He laughed at me. Thought it was hilarious."

"It probably was."

"Probably. But it stunk to high heaven. Huge mess."

"I'm laughing inside right now."

Julie watched Anastasia turn to grab a bag of edamame. "I'll bet you are."

"Mm."

"That's a lot of soybeans."

"I'm moving away from M&M's."

"I never see you eating M&M's."

"That's because I'm excellent at not sharing."

By the juices, Julie grabbed two attached two-quart bottles of carrot juice. "My other brother, Dave, loves carrot juice."

Anastasia stopped the cart and turned to Julie. "Tell me a story."

"Um. Okay. How about after LA when Tom took me to the Tehachapi Loop. Which was awesome. Talk about your elegant engineering solutions. If you—"

"No. Tell me a story, about you, that passes the Bechdel test."

"Well. Thursday I hung out with the Nut Caucus, a girls' engineering club."

"Great story."

"Although—hmm. The first time I met them we mostly talked about Tim."

"Tim."

"A guy."

"Obviously."

"Last time was triplanes and math."

"Exciting stuff."

"At least as exciting as Tim, that's for sure. Oo. Salami. You want one?"

"Sure."

Julie popped one in her mouth, dropped its toothpick in the trash, then drummed her temples with the tips of her fingers. For a moment, Anastasia again hated how beautiful she was. Her skin was perfect, her cheekbones so high. Every man they'd passed so far had checked her out. The lazy swing in her walk dripped sex and, best Anastasia could tell, it was entirely unconscious. She was built to attract men. And in some primal way, Anastasia despised the threat. And admired it. And feared it. She wished to emulate her. She wished to reject her, kick her to the curb, destroy her. This must be what it felt like to be an australopithecus. Or in the court of Louis XIV. Frickin Françoise-Athénaïs.

Charity.

Charity, Anastasia. Charity.

Yet the question still came out harsh. "So boys are the meaning of life then?"

Julie shrugged. "Aren't they? 'Families can be together forever.' 'No other success can compensate for failure in the home.' Don't they always say who you marry's the most important decision you'll ever make? Because the purpose of life is binding together the generations? And generations occur because boys and girls. You know."

"Have sex."

"Well, yeah. That. I was thinking of love but biologically what's the difference?"

Anastasia did not like the taste of Julie's logic. But she didn't have a ready rebuttal. So she said what Julie would probably call the ess-aitch word and followed it with "So boys are the meaning of life. What the hell am I doing studying Sanskrit?"

Julie walked over to her and took Anastasia's shoulders. Anastasia looked up to her face and fell into Julie's eyes. "Tell me about Sanskrit."

And, at that moment, Anastasia loved her.

In fact, she told Julie about Indo-European languages generally, spending a full five minutes on the various iterations of *poplar* over the Indo-European speaking world. Julie asked smart questions and Anastasia felt smarter being able to answer them. Although Anastasia mentioned a couple male scholars, it did not feel like they were talking about boys until she was reaching for tampons and the cart banged into the bordering Costco-sized boxes of Durex condoms and she froze midsentence as they crashed to the concrete.

"Why," said Julie, "are those always next to the tampons? Every store it's the same. This'll keep the real one from making you pregnant, and you plug that one in to celebrate not being pregnant. But! The very next item? Not here apparently but in drugstores across America? Pregnancy tests! In case you screw up, I have to imagine, since two of the three are about not being pregnant."

"You want to be pregnant?"

"No! Not particularly, I mean. Certainly not today. But, you know." Julie gestured at her midsection. "It's what I signed up for."

Anastasia drummed her fingers on the cart's handle. "You know how the twins won't shut up about us getting our cycles to sync up?"

Julie nodded.

"Why do they do that?"

Julie's gaze wandered up to the fluorescent lights far, far above. A finch flew past. Finally, "I see three options:

"First, they think it's a symbol of friendship and they want us all to be *so* close.

"Two, they're afraid on some primeval level and don't want to be alone.

"Three, they think it's cute in some unfathomable way."

Anastasia turned the tampons over in her hands. "Are— you afraid?"

"Freud says we are, doesn't he?"

"Screw Freud."

"Everyone else does."

"Well, I hope they use a condom. I do not want that misogynist pregnant."

Julie snorted and picked up the condoms. "What would happen if we just left these lying around the front room?"

"We should totally do that." Anastasia's mind filled with evil possibilities.

"How's the coat?"

"What?"

Julie pointed at her. "The coat. How do you feel? And do you want a gummy vitamin? They're giving them away over there."

"Oh." Anastasia looked down at herself. "I totally forgot I had it on. And no. I hate gummy stuff."

"Let's pass then. Forgot because you're totally comfortable in it or because you don't care anymore?"

"I'm—not sure."

Julie grabbed two more boxes of condoms from the floor. "Want to see me juggle?" Anastasia shrugged. Julie threw the boxes into the air. They tumbled right back to her feet. And she curtsied.

They worked their way upstream against the checkout

lines pushing their way through the store. "This is the bad thing about Saturdays," said Anastasia. "And we didn't even get over to the books. I'm going anyway. Hope you don't mind."

Julie handed her a small paper cup with a slice of energy bar in it.

"Thanks." Anastasia stuck it in her mouth. "I hate these things too."

"Me too," said Julie. "But we've already hit our quota of skipping free food today. We are college students, remember."

Anastasia spit it back into the cup and folded it closed.

Julie held out her cup; Anastasia deposited hers into Julie's who threw them away. "Why don't they hand out free broccoli, I wonder?"

"James Bond wouldn't approve."

"That sounds like the sort of joke my brother would tell," said Julie. "Which is to say I don't get it and doubt it's worth having explained. No offense."

"No, you're right." Anastasia pulled the cart sideways up to the table loaded with hardbacks. "No, no, no, no. . . ." She abandoned the cart and kept walking, tapping each title with a finger as she worked her way to the paperbacks.

Julie picked a garishly covered book with giant neon letters and read the back. Seemed someone got themselves murdered. Anastasia came rushing back holding a massive tome called *The Historian* in front of her, accelerating it towards Julie's face like a 3D jumpscare.

"I forgot about this! I meant to read it but never did! Someone must have returned this copy because it was alone, just buried under a bunch of 1776s!"

"What is it?"

"Well, it's a vampire book, but unlike Laurell, people say it's actually good for you!"

"Okay!"

"I'm totally getting this. Plus my apple pie and brie and I am *set* for the weekend. Listen to this: 'It is with regret that I imagine you, whoever you are' blah blah blah 'regret is partly. . . . If you are not my successor in some other sense you will soon be my heir. . . .' okay, whatever. Anyway, she inherits a bunch of paperwork and documentation and stuff about Bram Stoker's *Dracula* only it's real and a family secret or something. I'm not sure. Anyway, I'm getting it."

Julie leaned her head back on her neck. "That maybe sounds interesting?"

"Well." Anastasia dumped the book next to the tampons and folded her arms. "You can have a slice of pie, but no touching my book till I've finished it."

"Fair enough. Does she wear a trenchcoat?"

"No idea. You still want to look at chocolate?"

Julie shook her head. "I've had so many little hunks o' cheese and sausage, and cups of cashews and yogurt and noodles, that I'm not sure I'll even need dinner tonight."

"Unless it's free."

"Of course. Always room for one more sample." Julie looked back the way they had come. "Should have taken that gummy vitamin. I'll go grab us some. At least to get this taste out of our mouths."

"So long as they don't look like Superman. Bechdel rule, remember." Anastasia pushed the cart backwards into the main stream. "Do you have a checkout-picking strategy?"

"You mean knowing which is fastest? Rather than just shortest?"

"Right."

Julie nodded. "Avoid grandmas. Most likely to pay by check. One person with a ton of stuff is better than a ton of people with a couple items each. Moms with small kids will do all they can to get the heck out of Dodge." She shrugged. "But with lines this long it's a total crapshoot. I'll go get us the little-girl gummies."

Anastasia watched Julie walk away, an exact replica of the slomo boomchickywonk walk from every crude comedy she'd seen in her debauched high-school career. Except unlike a trampy actress in sex-inch stilettos, Julie was merely walking her walk, then raising her arms (and everything else) as she turned sideways to slide between two carts. Anastasia looked down at herself, expecting to be disappointed. Instead she saw sharp black lines, reaching nearly to the floor. For a moment she was outside her body, viewing her profile from a distance. She was Van Helsing. Add a decent hat and she would have a silhouette distinguishable from space. She was a slayer. She was a rockstar. She was Anastasia Motherfreaking Taylor, human god.

She took the coat off. Folded it carefully. Caressed its lapels. Looked at her copy of *The Historian*. And flung the coat onto a display of toboggans.

Her line moved forward. Anastasia turned, and followed.

Meet Julie Them

SATURDAY AFTERNOON

Julie skipped out of Anastasia's car and looked at the peak of Brick House's roof. For a moment she had—it was almost as if—

"Oh! Julie?"

She turned around and a boy she didn't recognize was peering up at her through a pair of Coke bottles. "Mm?"

"Are you busy tonight?"

Julie looked over his head and into the sky, and thought. "I—can't remember. It's Saturday. It certainly seems likely."

Anastasia grabbed her newly shopped items and slammed the car door. "See you inside."

"Yeah . . ." She looked back down at the boy, his eyes distorted by those lenses. "C'mon in. I'll see if I can figure out what I'm doing."

SATURDAY EVENING

Julie sat disassembling the complimentary bread from its bowl, pressing the bits into cubes and building a wall. She was trying to remember how she knew the boy in front of her. Did they go to church together? Was he an engineer? Was he a friend of one of her roommates? She liked how his wiry premature combover, white shirt and tie, and eye-warping eyeglasses turned him into a '60s-era NASA nerd and she liked the width of his shoulders and the way he hesitated before speaking and the way he didn't seem to be trying that much to impress her.

But she didn't know his name.

And it seemed rude to ask.

SUNDAY MORNING

Julie was getting dressed for church when a knock at her bedroom door interrupted her. She left off buttoning her blouse and opened the door.

Jill was there and immediately dropped her eyes. "Sorry— I thought—I thought you'd be— Would you like to walk with me? Or are you getting a ride?"

"Walking would be great." Julie finished her blouse and grabbed her purse—first slipping in pens, pencils, socket wrench from her backpack—then scriptures.

SUNDAY AFTERNOON

Julie turned down several offers for rides and walked home with Jill. A handful of boys followed them to the edge of the building, five or six all the way to the stairs at the edge of campus, and three all the way down to the street.

"By the way, I'm Jarvis," said one.

"Oh, yeah! I'm Miguel."

"Uh, Spencer. Spencer Jun."

It occurred to Julie that, at that moment, she was likely part of the most diverse fivesome in all of Utah. The girls black and white. The boys two shades of brown and one shade of yellow. She figured this realization was either utterly racist or utterly enlightened. Not much room in the middle. She'd have to ask Jill.

SUNDAY EARLY EVENING

Jill leaned back on the couch and pulled her ankles toward her body. "When my family—my second family—moved to Montana, I didn't see a nonwhite person for six months. Two Native kids went to high school with me. A Mexican family moved in my sophomore year—the oldest brother asked me to prom that year."

Anastasia muttered something from behind *The Historian.* Julie ignored her. "Did you go?"

"I said yes, but he got sick and we didn't end up going. I was relieved, honestly. I mean—I never wanted to go in the first place, but he'd been turning into a real—lothario—and I was afraid he had—ideas. Instead we never spoke again."

"Hang on," said Anastasia and put down her book to look at them. "How tall were you in tenth grade?"

"The same as now." Jill gestured at herself in a way that

seemed to emphasize the flatness of her chest. "I've been about the same since seventh grade."

"Huh." She went back to reading.

Julie rode the pause for a while. "How's the book?"

"Really good."

Julie looked at Jill who smiled and ducked her head.

SUNDAY NIGHT

The twins had arranged for ward prayer to be at Brick House this week, so all the people they'd seen at church that morning were crammed into their living room—an excellent opportunity to be forced to fling legs over neighbors, to be smashed so tight as to feel the entire length of another against you, to sit on the floor between someone else's legs—a regular Mormon orgy. Julie escaped into the kitchen while various announcements were made. Apparently the whole ward was going bowling together tomorrow night. Beth and Don were engaged; everybody go ahead and cheer and think hopefully about the person you're sitting next to right now; uncomfortable laughter. Temple-recommend interviews Tuesday night. A couple people called on missions. Devotional this week looks cool. Anyone on a CPA track? Could I talk to you afterwards? Driving to Logan on Friday if anybody wants to carpool. Lost a bracelet at church if anyone. . . .

They droned on and Julie sipped a glass of water. At every joke she could hear the twins laughing first and last. No sign of Jill or Anastasia. Soon the prayer would be said and those who regretted coming would bolt and the rest would stand and gladhand and flirt; boys would start trickling into the kitchen. Julie could try and sneak into her bedroom before that—no boy would dare cross the chastity line—but it was a coward's way out. So she placed her glass in the sink and folded her arms to meet the onslaught.

MONDAY MORNING

Jill leaned against the bathroom doorjamb watching Julie put on mascara.

"Why do you wear that?"

"What do you mean?"

Jill shrugged and looked away, mumbling into her shoulder. "You already have crazy lashes. You look—like a mascara commercial even without mascara."

"Uh." Julie finished and batted her eyes, then turned to Jill. "I like . . . the overthetopness of makeup. I like being the most beautiful clown every once in a while. As for mascara, why not? Anything that keeps eyes on the face must be good. You need in here?"

"Yeah."

"I'm done. Hang on." Julie snapped and flipped and screwed various cases and tubes and things and dumped them into her drawer, then touched Jill's shoulder with her hand as she squeezed past. "There you go."

MONDAY AFTERNOON

Julie stared blindly at her out-of-focus professor. Her conscious mind fought boldly in attempt to regain control but the only message to get through was *close your mouth*. She did and realized she had drooled ever so slightly. She rubbed the back of her hand against her chin and reapplied herself.

Monday Wednesday Friday were her busy days, four straight hours, 9am–1pm, with her major classes. She was studying two types of nutrition (early childhood and the adolescent years), money management, and the basics of home maintenance. The last one was a breeze. For a girl that had turned off the water and disassembled the kids'-bathroom sink at age six, not much here Julie didn't know. Listening now to a discussion on ensuring outlets are safely grounded was unendurable. But Julie had never intentionally skipped a class in her life and wasn't about to start now.

Until she was. She felt her face make an embarrassed apologetic smile. She gathered her things in her arms and grabbed her bag and . . . left.

And stood in the JFSB lobby, looking through its wall of windows onto campus. She fitted everything into her bag, threw it over her shoulder.

And walked.

MONDAY NIGHT

And arrived home at 10:30 where the twins were bubbling with a trio of boys over what bad bowlers they (the twins) were and what good bowlers they (the boys) were. Upon finishing this thought, they chattered over to Julie and demanded her whereabouts that evening to which she unhelpfully replied, "Bowling is a physics problem."

"What?"

"F=ma. Just throw in, you know, direction of, you know, all of that."

Two of the boys laughed in soft staccato confusion. The third turned back to Ashleigha. "But if you're such a poor bowler, why do you have your own shoes? And pink velcro! So cute and retro!"

The other boys amened, and Julie smiled and passed down the hall to her bedroom.

TUESDAY AFTERNOON

Julie sat frowning in the small anteroom before the counselors' offices and wondered what she was doing. She was supposed to be in her spinning class right now. Which made it one-and-a-half classes she'd ditched. In a row! No one else was here except the befreckled student secretary who kept forgetting why Julie was here.

"Sorry to bother you again." The student had two braided pigtails which she flipped between her fingers. "I'm really sorry. But it says you've already declared."

"That's right."

"And you're actually a bit ahead with the requirements for your major."

"True."

"So . . . *why* are you here?"

Julie sighed and looked at a motivational poster of skydivers making a snowflake on their way back to earth. "I just need to talk to a counselor."

"Okay, but why? They're really busy."

"I'm the only one here."

"That's because it's November." She flipped her pigtails with a toss of her head. "No one comes in November."

"Lucky for me?"

". . . I guess. You should really make an appointment first."

Julie stood and walked to the desk. "So what's her first available slot today?"

"She doesn't actually . . . have anyone . . . today. Not yet anyway."

"Then I'll take right now."

"But you don't even know why you're here?"

"Nevertheless."

The secretary exhaled so long Julie wondered if she might pass out, then she slapped the desk with both hands and pushed herself up. "I'll be right back."

Ninety-three seconds later, Julie was sitting in a trendy square plush chair and watching an overpermed and sharp-nosed profile type furiously. "Quite irregular to make an appointment the day of."

"I'm sorry. I've never tried to see a counselor before. I didn't know."

"Never seen—" The woman swiveled toward Julie and fixed her with owl eyes. "How do you ever anticipate graduating if that's the amount of planning you put into things? What's your ID number?"

Julie gave it to her then listened to some hems and haws then a begrudging,

"Well. You're a lucky one. You're doing just fine."

"Thank you."

"But shouldn't you be in spinning right now?"

"I hurt my ankle this morning," Julie lied to her surprise.

"Mm."

"I was wondering?"

"Yes."

"Can I—can I just add a minor? Or is there some special process?"

Owl Eyes narrowed them and looked Julie up and down. "What minor?"

"I'm—I'm interested in engineering?"

Owl Eyes chuckled. "First—I see here" tapping the screen "you passed both calculus AP tests—and that's lovely, it really is, but you haven't taken any math since then and—"

"I haven't? I should have two classes from my hometown CC that I took last summer. Are they not there?"

"Nnnnng." Tap tap. Click. "Hrm. Yes, I see them. But why engineering? Have you considered maybe drawing? That's a useful skill. I used to be quite adept at a pencil myself."

"What?"

"Or—you look fit—why not some dance classes? The dance minor is challenging but it's very healthful."

Julie couldn't reply and Owl Eyes took that as a yes.

"I could add it right now. Dance minor. Keep it general. Then you can try all types. There will be some performance obligations, but it's a great way to be seen as you can imagine."

Julie moved her head from side to side, as if looking for fruit to pick. She lifted her pink backpack to rifle through, to look for the engineering information she'd printed off the web. But she grabbed the wrong zipper and her reaching hand instead collided with a thin, cold, metal shaft. She pulled out her socket wrench.

She pulled it out, flipping and rolling it between her fingers like a baton.

". . . besides, the grace attendant to . . . to . . . to. . . . What is that?"

"It's a socket wrench."

"Yes, but—why?"

Julie pulled it close to her eyes. "You know. I've never thought to ask myself that before. 'Why.' It's a good question."

"So . . . I should put you down for the dance minor."

"No."

"No?"

"No." Julie spun the wrench around her thumb, dropping it into her hand like a Japanese gelpen. "No."

Owl Eyes sat back and crossed her arms. "Well I don't know *what* you came in for today."

"Neither did I. Quick question. How many credits in the MFHD minor? How close am I?"

"That's your major."

"I know. But if I changed it to a minor? How close am I?"

"You would have to audition for the dance major."

"How close?"

"Hhhhh." Click click. Tap. "You already have the credits. You just need one 300-level class. We are discontinuing the minor though. You would have to decide immediately and—"

"Okay. Let's do that."

"Seems a little unwise. Besides, you can't have a minor and no major."

"Civil engineering."

"What?" Owl Eyes widened them. "What? Who? You?"

Julie held up her socket wrench. "Why."

Owl Eyes humphed. "Make an appointment on your way out. Hopefully we can still fit you in when you realize your error."

"Thank you."

"Most engineers take five years to graduate. You're already a year behind."

"I'll double up. All homework all the time."

"But no one. You. Pink."

Julie leaned back in her tweed chair and waved the wrench in the air. "Do you have any idea how hard this major is going to be?"

Owl Eyes, softly, "No—"

Julie laughed like freezing, pure, spring runoff. "Me neither."

WEDNESDAY MORNING

Julie whistled her way into Early Childhood Nutrition and whipped out her notebook ready to go.

"You look happy today."

Julie turned to the girl next to her. "I am. I feel like I finally know why I'm here."

The girl buried her eyes under thick black eyebrows.

"Huh."

"Don't get me wrong—I will *never* regret taking this class, and no doubt it will prove plenty useful, but I feel weirdly free."

"Congratulations? Are you engaged or something?"

Julie held up her naked fingers, smiled, and said, "Something."

THURSDAY EVENING

Julie sat alone in room 245 of the Clyde Building putting numbers into a function that seemed an apt metaphor for changing majors halfway through sophomore year without having taken any of the prerequisites. She figured, as a metaphor, it was a success as she didn't seem able to make it through the other end without simple arithmetical errors.

The door crashed open and Julie glanced up to see Bets. "You came again," she said. "Be right back." And she left.

A few moments later, a string of a girl walked in. At least six foot, probably closer to six-six, her steps were long and arced, like Goofy in slow motion, giving her an otherworldly elegance, like the stretched image of a zero-gravity ballerina.

"You must be Julie—Ruth told me about you. I'm so glad you came back. Ruth said you would but Bets seemed less confident. I'm Sylvia."

"Hi, Sylvia." Julie stacked her papers and slid them into her backpack. "You're an engineering student too?"

"Grad student, yes. I'm back after a few years at a firm in Nashville. We specialize in bridges. Sadly, the government does not specialize in paying for bridges. Felt like we were just waiting for bridges to fall down." She sat on a metal stool about five feet from Julie. She put her feet on the upper rung and her knees pointed skyward nearing her chin, turning her into a series of acute angles. Reminded Julie of Charlotte A. Cavatica. Sylvia laid her elbows on her knees and made a nest with the back of her hands for her face to rest in. "But not you?"

Julie rewound the conversation in her mind. "Oh. No. Not yet. I'm halfway through changing majors."

"You are! Why?"

"I realized this is what I want to do. And that I can do what I want to do."

Sylvia nodded. "Makes sense. You'll have some catching up to do."

"I know."

"What year are you?"

"I'm a sophomore."

Sylvia lifted her neck. "Really? Somehow you seem . . . older. More . . . worldly. Not in the Mormon sense but in the way other people use it."

Julie shrugged. "You did your undergraduate here?"

"Mm."

"You felt well prepared?"

"Sure. Better than most of my peers, honestly. We have a good program here."

"Hi, Julie!" Ruth stood waving in the doorway, then she rushed over to give Julie and Sylvia hugs. "I'm so glad you came! I talked Sylvia into coming this week so she could meet you. What did you bring to work on?"

"Well, actually," said Julie. "I didn't bring any engineering problems, per se. More like—engineering-*school* problems."

"Oh! My gosh!" Ruth hugged Julie again then jumped up and down a couple times. "Am I overreacting? I might have completely misunderstood what you said!"

Sylvia laughed at her. "No. You didn't."

The door opened rather noisily. They turned to watch Amelia struggle through, taking off her peacoat as she walked and holding a box filled with—springs? Ruth hurried over to help.

"Um," said Amelia, nodding at the rest of them. "Quite a few of us today. Good to see you, Sylvia. Julia." Julie waved and Sylvia said thanks. "Is Bets coming?"

"Behind you."

"Ah! Hi! Great. Let's get started. I wish more people would come but, you know, so it goes."

Bets closed the door behind them and in a moment everyone was in a tight circle. Julie then, from her left, Ruth, Sylvia on her stool, Amelia, Bets; Bets sitting a little back and ruining the circle's regularity but looking comfortable in her plastic chair with her boots kicked up on the box of springs.

"So first," said Amelia. "I have a pretty trustworthy rumor that says Brother Martinez is going to need a new TA within a couple weeks."

Ruth gasped. "Why? What happened to Levi?"

Amelia shook her head. "Not Levi. That other kid. What's his name? The Chinese kid? The one with all the visa problems? Anyway, I guess the problems have reached a crisis. I don't know if he's leaving or just has to quit his job or what, but now's the time to let Brother Martinez know you're interested. I can't take it, obviously, but one of you should. Ruth? You were looking."

Ruth nodded sadly. "I was. But I just took a job at the Creamery. I can't quit so soon. That's flaky."

"Yeah, but—" Amelia flung her hands in the air. "This is a job that you will want on resumes and you'll learn stuff and . . . stuff."

"I know! But—I also get free ice cream!"

"Oh." Amelia paused. "Enough to share?"

Ruth nodded.

"Bets? You interested?"

Bets shrugged. "I heard you mostly grade freshmen assignments. Sounds like some circle of hell."

Ruth giggled. "Abandon all hope!"

"That's not the point, Bets," said Amelia wagging a finger at Bets's face. "It's all about the letter of recommendation you get at the end."

Bets sighed. "Fine. I'll ask him about it tomorrow after class. But I still hate his mustache."

"Excellent." Amelia leaned back on her stool and smiled. "The only other thing is I have a box of springs. No idea what I'll be doing with them. But it seems like a fun problem for the Nut Caucus to solve."

Ruth pointed at Julie. "But Julie."

"Julie—?" Amelia's brow creased. "Oh. Right. Did you bring something again? Can we do springs instead?"

"I hope so. But first?" Julie pulled her backpack onto her

lap and unzipped the main pocket. "So. I was intending to bring something math-heavy but this week's gotten a bit weird and now I really actually need your help."

Amelia creased one eye. "How so?"

"Okay." Julie looked around the circle. Opening her mouth again would make it real. "Okay."

Sylvia reached out to her, then turned her palm upwards. "It's okay, Julie. Smile."

Julie tried to, held it, then smiled. "I'm changing majors. But I'm not exactly sure civil's the right choice—is structural a major on its own? Should I surprise myself and go mechanical? Mechanical sounds fun. Plus, I need faculty to sign off before the counselor will bite and I don't know who to go to."

Silence—until Bets said "Shut up!" then it broke apart. Ruth gave Julie another hug then threw her into Bets's lap. Amelia sat mouth agape. When Ruth's chattering died down, Julie resat herself and pulled a folder from her backpack.

"Hang on," said Amelia. "You can't just switch into engineering like that. These majors are hard. They're competitive! They're just letting you in? Like that?"

Bets pointed. "Tell her, Sylvia."

"Tell her what?"

"How hard it is to build respect."

Sylvia shrugged, lifting her spider arms into the air. "It's true. We have to be perfect. Unassailable."

Bets nodded. "No chinks in our lady armor."

"And it's worse if you're pretty." Sylvia tilted her head toward Amelia.

Ruth interrupted. "But everyone knows Amelia's the smartest undergrad we got."

"Exactly," said Bets.

Julie took a moment to look at each face. Ruth's welcomed and loved and hoped but glanced down. Sylvia's remained open but was almost too frank. Amelia's was half-hidden by her hair. Bets's moved slowly from side to side.

"I understand." Julie put her elbows on her knees and leaned forward. "That's why I need your help."

Amelia moved her head up slightly and Julie reached out and parted her hair like a veil. Half Amelia's mouth smirked and half smiled. "You're crazy, you know."

"I know." Julie released the rest of her breath. "Or now I do. I didn't know when we first met. I thought I was just an engineering groupie—not an engineering aspirant."

"What changed?"

Julie thought. A long time.

Bets checked her watch.

"Me. I changed."

Amelia nodded. "Okay. How can we help?"

She asked about the differences in career options when majoring in mechanical engineering versus industrial engineering—only to decide neither was right. She listened to advice and experience. She learned of this professor's habits and that professor's predilections. Who listened and who knew whom and who would get you on real projects. How to spend a summer in Singapore or Brazil or Louisiana. She took notes until she'd filled fifteen sheets of college-ruled.

The Nut Caucus meeting went late, springs forgotten, and it wasn't until she was putting her key in the Brick House lock that Julie realized she'd never asked Amelia if she'd gone out again with that boy.

SATURDAY NIGHT

Julie spent the day crosslegged on the couch cramming trig (not her favorite) and brushing off boys. Finally Ashleigha and Maddysyn left with two in tow—and Anastasia disappeared with one as well—leaving Julie and Jill alone. Julie paused to turn off most of the lights to limit the odds of an unexpected knock at the door and grabbed a fresh piece of paper to sully.

"You seem different," said Jill from the floor. "You're working different, I mean. More focused? More hungry."

Julie looked up, bit her pen. "That's very astute."

Jill lay on her stomach and turned to look at her. "Thank you."

Julie set the pen on her papers and pulled them onto her lap. "Come sit by me."

Jill did.

"I don't know why I'm being so secretive. If I want anyone to know, it's you."

Jill nodded.

"I am officially, no kidding, no reconsidering, no turning back, changing majors next week. Civil engineering. I'm going to have a miserable couple semesters while I catch up. I'll stay on for both spring and summer. I'm going to be too busy for any of the stuff I usually do. I fear I'm making a terrible mistake and I'm insanely giddy. Seriously. Instead of approximating happy, I *am* happy. I can't wait to start."

Jill took her in, and Julie noticed that deep in her coal eyes were wisps of viper green. Jill nodded and Julie exhaled in a big rush of joy.

"It feels so good to say it!"

Jill opened her arms and Julie pulled her in and pulled her up, spilling papers as they danced across the room. When they passed near the cd player Julie reached out and hit play and some random mix from some random boy started playing—a song carefully calibrated to be vaguely hopeful and mostly cool and trying just hard enough. Then the shuffle switched to a different cd and a dance remix of Franz Ferdinand started playing. They flung their arms and legs through the air till they were tired and plopped to the couch. Julie pushed her book and papers to the floor, and Jill leaned into her, put her head on Julie's shoulder, just as the shuffle switched to something a little more earnest—a well-meaning white boy and his guitar.

As he whined his sincerity, Julie felt Jill's body relax into hers and for a moment she knew how boys feel when someone small and vulnerable and lovely relaxed, and instinct suggested she bend her neck and kiss her friend. But at the same time she knew it wasn't what Jill needed and would be cruel besides. So instead she squeezed her shoulder and said, "Tonight we celebrate unplanned-for futures," and Jill said, "Amen," and Julie said, "I have tapioca," and they hugged and both found what they needed in that hug.

SUNDAY MORNING

Julie sits on a folding chair crammed into the back of an auditorium with two things on her mind. First, background, the metal trays passing back and forth carrying bread-and-water reminders of who she says she is, of what she believes but could think more about. Jill's black hand picking up a bit of white bread makes Julie think of Noah releasing the dove. He whom God loves releasing the symbol of God's love in trust that God's love will thus be made manifest.

Or, to quote every animal movie ever, if you really really love it, let it go.

If it doesn't come back, it was never yours anyway.

Second, the chair ahead of her. Just a simple folding chair, very few pieces, perfectly functional. Julie deconstructs the manufacturing process. Based on one of Amelia's textbooks she's been reading, how would the bars be welded together? In what order were things attached? How often are humans directly involved? Do you put the rubber feet on before or after connecting the two chair halves? How do you pack them to minimize both shipping costs and damage during transport?

The water arrives and Julie holds up her small paper cup before drinking and thinks of the Saints arriving in the Great Basin and starting one of history's great acts of irrigation. She imagines the water falling from the sky, traveling down watershed to reservoir, piped into a treatment facility, traveling to BYU, passing through a faucet and into this cup, being blessed and sanctified to her soul that she would remember the blood of her Brother and witness that she remembers him, will always remember him.

She places the cup to lips perfect as God ever made, and the water bleeds into her mouth and down her throat and into her soul.

She pulls the cup back, a slight touch of pink left behind where it touched her. She smashes it between thumb and forefinger, drops it into the used slot, and stares at her hands in her lap.

"Into my soul," she whispers. "My soul."

A chill passes down her arms.

"Julie Them's soul."

She looks up at the chair before her. In it sits a redhaired kid with a skunkspot; he's a bit overweight and has a limp she's never asked him about.

"Into his soul. As he partook of it."

She reaches to each side and takes a hand of Anastasia's and a hand of Jill's. "To our souls," she whispers.

"What?"

"Shh."

They listen to the occasional cup dropping into a tray, the shuffling of papers and skirts, the clearing of a throat or seven.

Julie notices Jill staring straight ahead and slightly up. A glance to the other side and, yes, Anastasia too. So Julie looks straight ahead and slightly up and catches a sunbeam. Motes dance in chaos up and down and lateral. Diagonal and orthogonal. One larger bit of fluff suddenly plummets upward and out of the light. She follows it in her imagination, flitting her eyes over the congregation and the industrial carpet and the men in suits sitting up front. She squeezes her neighbors' hands and smiles.

For are we not, she imagines some ancient poet saying, motes all in the eye of a loving, unblinking God?

MONDAY MORNING

Before walking to campus and making everything official, Julie walks a half a mile in the wrong direction to a hardware store and buys a set of sockets for her wrench. The costliest available. Round and smooth and clean and ready for action. She refuses a bag and opens the package, attaches the quarter-inch to her wrench and sticks it in her backpocket before thrusting the rest in her backpack and walking away.

The cashier watches her hardware all the way out the door, then turns to his buddy. "What the hell was that?"

"Dude," says his buddy. "A little respect?"

And their moment of silence fills the vacuum she's left behind.

Acknowledgments and such

I first attempted a Julie-in-2005 novel before 2005. So this has been a long road. First shoutout to Fob who've accompanied me on this path since before the beginning and who were the first to read a rough draft. Extra appreciation to Arwen and Danny for, you know, being cool. They didn't have to let me go all *hommage vampirique* on them.

Fob tried to talk me out of a lot of things and the book is immensely better for their feedback. The remaining flaws (and thanks in advance to Twitter for making a big deal about them) are all mine.

Maddie Pine and Kimberley Bocanegra were invaluable during the writing of the first full draft of this novel ten years ago. I don't think they know it, but they made it possible. You were awesome. Come say hi sometime because I bet you still are.

Therese Doucet first published *Byuck* in 2012. Seeing that book in print let me move past it—and provided the motivation to do so. Julie's first draft then took just a few weeks, but it was Therese's faith in her older brother that made that possible.

Researching Provo's 2005 music scene would have been impossible without the help of Chris Coy. Just as I needed the help he a) wrote back and b) was putting all *his* period podcast's episodes on YouTube. Good luck typing it on your first try, but do check these out:

https://www.youtube.com/playlist?list=PLCC4971BD22D29D04

More recently, Piper Anderson and Jakob Spjut came to my mathematical rescue. Extra thanks to Jakob for remaking those formulas in LaTeX so they could reproduce properly in print.

Thanks to the BCC Press team. They're several of the very best things to happen to Mormon lit in our lifetime. Nods to Michael and Cece and Conor and Holly and Jon and Andrew. And thanks, Matt, for making the two covers reveal a family resemblance.

Thanks also to everyone who read the entire book just to blurb it for me, but a special shoutout to Darlene who, even after everyone had edited the book a time or three, found a sentence whose ambiguous grammar suggested Julie was flashing people. *So* glad you caught that, Darlene!

Finally, thanks to Dave Them for being totally cool about not showing up in his sister's book. He even gave her a piece of business I'd been heartbroken to remove from his own. Now *that's* a good brother.

Hey, everybody. Wasn't that something? Good ol' Julie.

Anyway, you must be wondering what happens in the Them family saga prior to the events of *Just Julie's Fine* and boy oh boy do I have good news for you! I've invented a time machine!

Yup, thmadscientist at your service. All you have to do is turn the page and you'll be transported to the world of Julie's brother Dave in the year 2000, back when the future was still totally gonna happen.

Enjoy your trip! And don't step on any butterflies!

To Build a Fence

A public service message from
The Institute for Marital Concerns
Brigham Young Chapter
© 2000

As all you RM gospel scholars know, Brigham Young once said:

> I will give each of the young men in Israel, who have arrived at an age to marry, a mission to go straightway and get married to a good sister, fence a city lot, lay out a garden and orchard and make a home. This is the mission that I give to all young men in Israel.

This presents us with a distinct problem, if we 1) do not want to get married, 2) don't want to get married, or 3) would really rather not get married. If this sounds like you, then rest assured that we at the IMC are here to help you get out of what, at first glance, seems like a direct commandment from a prophet of God to get married.

Living in the post-Clinton era as we do, we have the right to demand strict word definitions and to nit-pick on how they fit together. Being exactly the sort of "Young Man in Israel" that Brigham Young was speaking both to and about, it is necessary to build excuses for ourselves. But a bad excuse is self-damnation and really good excuses are hard to come by in this dispensation of the fullness of times; so in order to stall for time, we need to demand some definitions while we strive to understand the "deeper" meaning of this prophetic utterance.

To the neophyte, defining "straightway" may seem our best starting point, but like any bomb, picking the wrong wire (or in this case, *word*) can make the whole thing go off in your face. Be warned: "Straightway" is such a potent word that it may, in fact, actually be impossible to completely disarm. In cases like this, where the obvious is not the ideal, it is wise to open the abstract mind, allowing fresh, clean and clear thoughts to fall in from above like so many bird droppings.

In the case of this phrase ("go straightway and get married"), the best place to start is probably "get." To those unfamiliar with the fine art of advanced word refinement, or *clarification*, "get" may not seem so great, but as every wise word clarificator knows, "get" is the word clarificator's best friend. For one thing, it is of that rare tribe of word safe to look up in the dictionary! Dozens upon dozens of wildly disparate definitions for the choosing! "Get" can make a sentence mean anything you please! "Go straightway and succeed in coming or going married!" "Go straightway and achieve as a result of military activity married!" "Go straightway and be subjected to married!" (Er. Bad example.)

But before we get *too* happy about discovering "get" just where it could have best been found, let's look at a larger portion of Brother Brigham's sticky speech:

> I will give each of the young men in Israel, who have arrived at an age to marry, a mission to go straightway and get married to a good sister, fence a city lot, lay out a garden and orchard and make a home.

All right, clarificators, here we go! First of all, why do we *need* to refine this statement? Because it is presenting us with a *mission*—or, in other words, it's handing out (heaven help us) *responsibility*; and if there is one thing we *don't* need (or at least *want*), it's responsibility! Brigham *couldn't* have meant for us to have *more* responsibility! We've had enough of that! We're RMs! Are you with me? ARE YOU *WITH* ME?!?!

BUT WAIT—*who* is he giving this mission to?

> . . . each of the young men in Israel, who have arrived at an age to marry . . .

Ah ha! There's an out right there! Who's to say what "an age to marry" is? Or whether we have "arrived" at such an age? I don't know, but I'm *sure* that doesn't include me!

But that's *too* easy, and not completely satisfactory. Here's why: I can't go around saying "I haven't 'arrived at an age to marry' yet" all of my life. Also, unless I can point to what I *am* doing to *obey* President Young rather than my reasons (however valid) for *not* obeying him, then the focus will remain on what I'm *not* doing and no amount of pious explication is likely to save me from the judgmental frowns of others. So let's look once again at this quote of Brother Brigham's, and this time, let's pay Close Attention to the *commas*:

> [The mission is] to go straightway and get married to a good sister, fence a city lot, lay out a garden and orchard and make a home.

It doesn't take a prophet to realize that President Young has offered us young men in Israel who've arrived at an age to marry three options:

1. Go straightway and get married to a good sister
2. Fence a city lot
3. Lay out a garden and orchard and make a home

The first option is what we kinda wanna avoid and the third is an awful lot of hard work. Therefore, the only option I can see left for us (short of apostasy) is to fence a city lot. If we can get oh, say, six thousand of us young men in Israel together some Saturday afternoon, we should be able to fence a city lot in no time! And then we can go home knowing we have been faithful in following the commands of the prophets! A major plus of this plan is that we will be able to carry around a Polaroid of our fenced city lot—our pride and joy—to show anyone who may ask us why the only ring we're wearing is our well-worn CTR.

"You see, Brother XYZ," we might say, "while *you* were off getting married to a good sister, *I* did the thing most wouldn't. *I* built a fence." That should shut them up.

And hey! It almost sounds heroic!

Simple Faith

David Them had not expected "To Build a Fence" to be such a success. He had thought it was funny when they wrote it, but never imagined it would fly out of control like it did.

His roommate Curses thought the wild reactions were great and wanted to turn their essay into a book. Dave didn't necessarily disagree, but he didn't really think they could write a book in one crazy evening like they had "To Build a Fence." He also didn't figure that one freak hit necessarily meant there was a book market for smart-alecky, byucky commentary.

"To Build a Fence" reached its first audience when Curses read it at a ward party. Everyone loved it. Several of the guys asked for an electronic copy to electronically mail to their electronic friends, and before the week was out someone had emailed Dave a copy of "this hilarious new thing going around email." By the end of the month *The Daily Universe* had done an investigative report on who the authors really were. The reporter was Curses's older sister's former roommate, and the story had been Curses's idea, but the story inspired a spate of controversy over the appropriateness of the essay's sentiment. For almost three weeks, the letters to the editor page was bogged down with wildly disparate commentary. Dave's favorite letter made the inevitable suggestion that those who want to build fences would be better off attending another university. His second favorite was a failed but heartwarming attempt to start a fence-building club.

Simultaneously, both Dave and Curses started getting email from people they had never met. Apparently their fellow students were taking the news story, looking them up in the BYU directory and finding their email addresses. They received date offers and accolades from people who had liked the essay, and self-righteous ramblings and confused threats from people who had not liked it.

Dave had been too freaked out by the bulk of attention to write back, but Curses had used the text from the emails he received as content for the new "To Build a Fence" website he set up with help from their roommate Peter, a computer science major always on the lookout for some new bait in his endless quest to attract the fairer sex to the apartment.

After everything calmed down, Curses dropped the book idea but made a suggestion that actually appealed to Dave—it seemed much easier. What about writing a play?

That evening, Dave's hometown friend Martha "Referee" Plantree dropped by right after lacrosse practice; her longish, brownish hair was still wet from the shower. She often stopped by since Dave's apartment complex, Draftwood, right next to the westernmost stadium parking, was across University Avenue from Sierra de Provost, where

Ref lived, right between the intramural fields and Wyview. But late fall? And with wet hair? All the way from campus? Dave shook his head and tut-tutted.

"You really shouldn't be walking around in the cold with your hair like that, Ref," he said. "I told you I'd give you a ride if you needed one."

"Thanks, Mom," she said. "Is Peter here?"

"No."

"Good. Then I'll come in." She walked in and whipped her wet hair so it hit Dave in the face. "Hey, Curses."

Curses waved. "Hey, Ref. Nice smack."

"Thanks. What are you guys up to?"

"We're writing a play."

"Oh no. About building fences?"

Dave shut the door and walked back into the conversation. "Ha ha ha. No."

"What then?"

"Actually," Curses said as he moved some papers off the red and blue plaid couch to make room for a lady, "it's Dave's idea."

"Oh? What is this idea, Dave?"

"The idea," Dave said, pausing to clear his throat artistically, "is that there are people out to despoil the dreams and ambitions of young people, the ones still unjaded by the worldliness of the world. They're called the Pragmati."

"Scary."

"Isn't it great?" asked Curses. "The play was my idea, but this Pragmati thing is fantastic. Of course, it's a love story at heart."

"Of course," said Ref, "love being your expertise. When did you guys decide to write a play?"

"Recently. But it is a love story. Also: it's a mystery." Curses glanced over his shoulders then whispered, "We know all about mysteries."

Dave sat down on the floor, across from Curses and Ref. "It's a terrifying mystery, too. I don't know who's actually part of the Pragmati and who's just been brainwashed by their soul-stealing antics, propaganda and whatnot, but I do know that their power on campus is strong. Take a look at the letters-to-the-editor page."

Ref gave Dave a look and uncrossed her arms. "Is this a play about BYU? And wouldn't secret combinations be against the Honor Code?"

"Yes and good question. I don't think they're specifically mentioned. Curses?"

"Not that I can remember. But there must be some sort of 'other' category it would fall under."

"You would think so." Dave gasped. "Unless—unless—unless the Honor Code Office has been infiltrated! What if they have become the enforcing arm of the Pragmati! Oh my!"

"This is getting better all the time," said Curses.

"Oh my yes," Ref said as she rested her head on the back of the couch.

"And maybe those who continue to dare to dream—"

"Like yourself?" asked Curses.

"Like myself, are turned over to the Honor Code Office to be 'dealt with' and 'dismissed.'"

"Yikes," said Curses.

"You guys will never get this produced on campus if you're accusing the Honor Code Office of secret combinations."

Dave looked at her. "Are you saying you're Pragmati?"

Ref smiled that smile girls smile when they think they're being naughty. "Maybe."

Curses: "Now I'm really yikesing."

Ref turned to him. "Okay, Texas boy, what's your major?"

"Communications."

"Exactly. And you, Dave?"

"English. You know that."

"I did, but I'm proving a point. The Pragmati have won over us all. We're not in our most majoriest of majors. I should be with a musician and a writer right now, not a communicator and an Englisher. Sellouts."

"Right, but see, we're writing a play. It's rebellion against the Pragmati—following our dreams, et cetera. We've started living the dream."

"Oh, I gotcha." Ref put her feet up on the hot-chocolate table. "I just read an article that said Christian death metal is rebellion against our secular society."

"Did it have a pie chart?" asked Curses.

"No."

"Never believe anything in a magazine that does not have an accompanying pie chart."

Dave sighed and turned to Curses. Sometimes it was so hard to hold a serious conversation with him in the room. "Curses, you're crazy."

"Me, Curses? Crazy? Curses Olai, crazy? Curses?"

"Do you see anyone else here named Curses?"

"No, but curiously enough, there is another Curses on campus. She's from Jamaica."

"Really?" Ref asked.

"Maybe."

"So you made it up."

"No! Her name is Curses Maybe."

"Really?" she asked again.

"Sure!"

"I don't believe you."

"Well, you may be right," Curses conceded. "She may be graduated by now."

"Anyway," said Dave, putting equal emphasis on the *any* and the *way*, "this isn't Christian death metal, but, um, Mormon rock opera. And besides, it's not rebellion. Rebellion is petty and childish. This is art and education."

"Whatever you say, of course," said Ref. "What do you call it? *Madame Pragmati*?"

"What? No, it's called *Byuck: A Rock Opera*."

"What's Byuck?"

"It's like BYU, only it's Byuck."

"I don't get it."

Dave looked at Curses and Curses shrugged. "No one does," said Dave.

"Then why are you calling it something no one gets?"

Dave opened his mouth a few times. Finally he said, "Simple faith."

Theric Jepson chewed on more pens as a college sophomore than he does now, using his canines to cut them into spirals and broomends. Perhaps because, in those days, he did not have a laptop?

Speaking of our technological past, while Julie not having a cellphone is appropriate for her character, Theric admits it also made her easier to write. Julie didn't have a phone in 2005; Theric still doesn't have one in 2023. Which either makes him an inspiring icon or extremely annoying.

You are welcome to your own opinion, of course, but he likes to imagine Julie thinks he's cool.

But everyone likes to imagine Julie thinks they're cool.

That's just the effect she has on people.

Made in United States
Orlando, FL
05 November 2023

38574151R00104